PRAISE FOR THE NOVELS OF
KATIE MacALISTER

Memoirs of a Dragon Hunter
"Bursting with the author's trademark zany humor and spicy romance . . . this quick tale will delight paranormal romance fans."—*Publishers Weekly*

Sparks Fly
"Balanced by a well-organized plot and MacAlister's trademark humor."—*Publishers Weekly*

It's All Greek to Me
"A fun and sexy read."—The Season for Romance
"A wonderful lighthearted romantic romp as a kick-butt American Amazon and a hunky Greek find love. Filled with humor, fans will laugh with the zaniness of Harry meets Yacky."—*Midwest Book Review*

Much Ado About Vampires
"A humorous take on the dark and demonic."—*USA Today*
"Once again this author has done a wonderful job. I was sucked into the world of Dark Ones right from the start and was taken on a fantastic ride. This book is full of witty dialogue and great romance, making it one that should not be missed."—Fresh Fiction

The Unbearable Lightness of Dragons
"Had me laughing out loud. . . . This book is full of humor and romance, keeping the reader entertained all the way through . . . a wondrous story full of magic. . . . I cannot wait to see what happens next in the lives of the dragons."—Fresh Fiction

Also By Katie MacAlister

Dark Ones Series
A Girl's Guide to Vampires
Sex and the Single Vampire
Sex, Lies, and Vampires
Even Vampires Get the Blues
Bring Out Your Dead (Novella)
The Last of the Red-Hot Vampires
Crouching Vampire, Hidden Fang
Unleashed (Novella)
In the Company of Vampires
Confessions of a Vampire's Girlfriend
Much Ado About Vampires
A Tale of Two Vampires
The Undead in My Bed (Novella)
The Vampire Always Rises
Enthralled
Desperately Seeking Vampire
Axegate Walk

Dragon Sept Series
You Slay Me
Fire Me Up
Light My Fire
Holy Smokes
Death's Excellent Vacation
(short story)
Playing WIth Fire
Up In Smoke
Me and My Shadow
Love in the Time of Dragons
The Unbearable Lightness of Dragons
Sparks Fly
Dragon Fall
Dragon Storm
Dragon Soul
Dragon Unbound
Dragonblight
You Sleigh Me

Dragon Hunter Series
Memoirs of a Dragon Huner
Day of the Dragon
A Confederacy of Dragons

Born Prophecy Series
Fireborn
Starborn
Shadowborn

Time Thief Series
Time Thief
Time Crossed (short story)
The Art of Stealing Time

Matchmaker in Wonderland Series
The Importance of Being Alice
A Midsummer Night's Romp
Daring in a Blue Dress
Perils of Paulie

Papaioannou Series
It's All Greek to Me
Ever Fallen in Love
A Tale of Two Cousins
Acropolis Now

Contemporary Single Titles
Improper English
Bird of Paradise (Novella)
Men in Kilts
The Corset Diaries
A Hard Day's Knight
Blow Me Down
You Auto-Complete Me

Noble Historical Series
Noble Intentions
Noble Destiny
The Trouble With Harry
The Truth About Leo

Paranormal Single Titles
Ain't Myth-Behaving

Mysteries
Ghost of a Chance
The Stars That We Steal From the
Night Sky

Steampunk Romance
Steamed
Company of Thieves

THE STARS THAT WE STEAL FROM THE NIGHT SKY

A NOVEL OF THE AKASHIC LEAGUE

KATIE MACALISTER

Cover by Croco Designs
Formatting by Racing Pigeon Productions

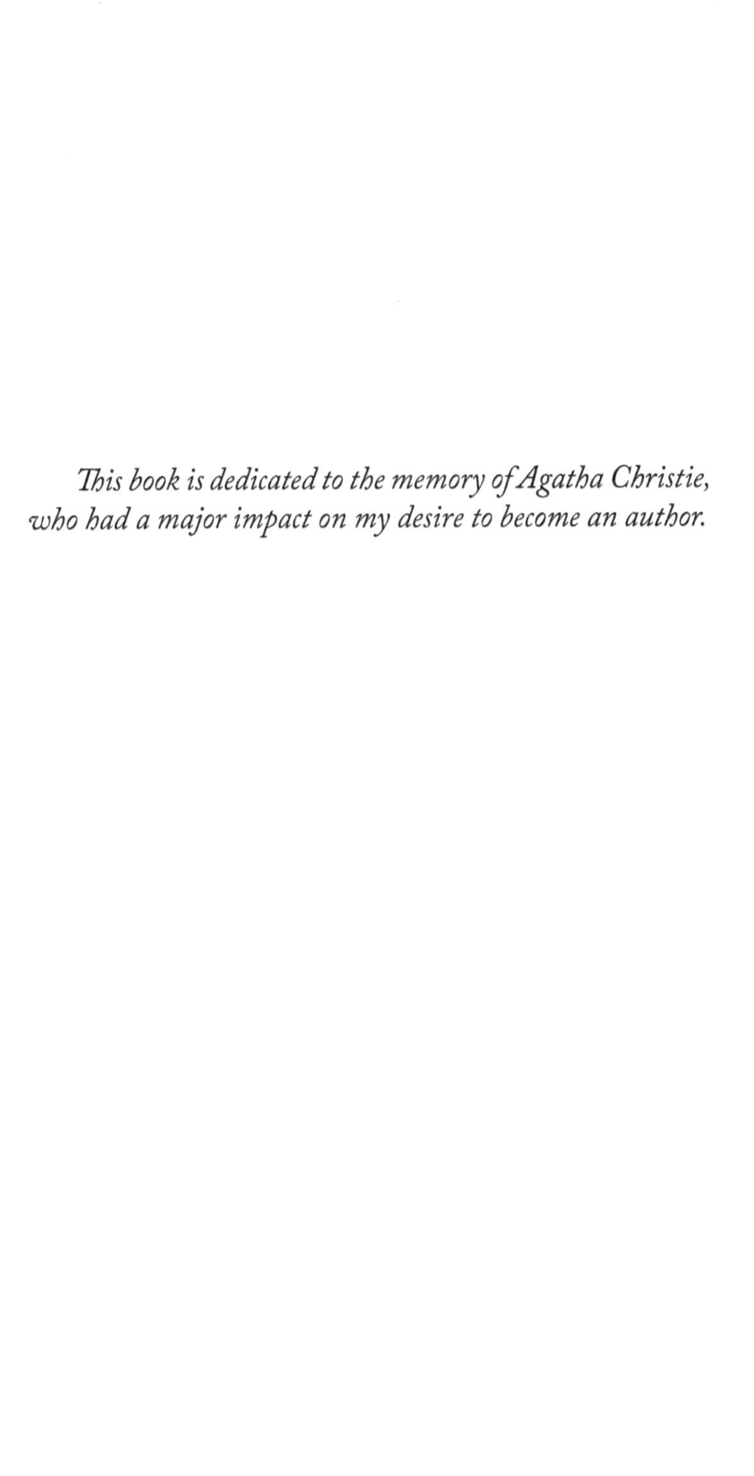

This book is dedicated to the memory of Agatha Christie, who had a major impact on my desire to become an author.

ONE

"So, are you, like, in trouble again? Are they going to put you in a creepy Otherworld jail and throw away the key? Torture you? Curse you?" Pixie, my sixteen-year-old foster child, eyed me with undisguised interest and, I suspected, a bit of glee. "Will they banish you to the Akasha so that you have to live in perpetual torment, driven mad by the fact you killed people?"

I took a deep, deep breath and gathered up my purse, checking to make sure that my phone had charged up enough to use it in an emergency. Electronic devices, as a rule, didn't like me. "We are not skipping therapy this week. I don't care how crampy you are—you clearly need to have time with your therapist if you are imagining that the Akashic League wants to torture and curse me. It's a meet and greet, Pixie, that's all. The new head honcho is meeting with all the members, and it's my turn to go in and hold my tongue while he spouts what is sure to be an inordinate amount of bullcrap. So no, I won't be banished, although living in perpetual torment is a very real possibility."

I gave her a long look that had her turning away quickly, but not quickly enough that I didn't see her grin. "Are you OK on your own, or do you want me to call my dad to keep you company?"

"Deus!" she swore, spinning around to glare at me, all four hands on her hips, her hair, which resembled two shiny black porcupines plopped on the top of her head, apparently bristling in response. "Do you think I need a babysitter? I'm sixteen, Karma, not an infant."

I held up a hand to stop her before she got on a roll. "Right, I'm sorry if I implied you were unable to stay at home by yourself. I just thought you might like the company, but if you don't, then I'll go. I should be back by dinnertime. Do you want to cook tonight, or should I?"

Pixie had a volatile personality at best, but given her life before coming to me, it was no surprise that she was touchy about anything regarding what she deemed an insult to her autonomy. However, we'd recently discovered that she greatly enjoyed experimenting with recipes, and had turned out to be a more than competent cook. "What were you going to make?" she asked, her eyes narrowed, hands still on hips.

"Mac and cheese?" I said, racking my brain.

"Dude," she said, waving that away with a dismissive gesture. "Anyone can make mac and cheese. I'll do a white cheddar and Gruyère truffle macaroni gratin. I've been dying to try that truffle oil you bought."

"Sounds good. I'll stop by the store on my way home and pick up some things for a salad," I said, then paused at the refrigerator, opening the vegetable bin, asking the dada (vegetable spirit) that resided there, "Do you have any preferences for salad fixings?"

He scrunched up his face for a few seconds before snapping his fingers. "I've been craving a Greek salad. Can we do that?"

"Of course. Anything else?"

"Arugula," he said, then sat back and patted a package of baby carrots. "These will hold me over until then. Thanks, Karma."

"No problem. Right, I'm off, then." I closed the fridge and went through the living room, Pixie trailing after me, her phone in one hand, obviously looking up recipes. I glanced over at the doggy playpen with zip-on lid that we had set up in front of the TV, which was playing at a low volume. "The imps can have one more hour of that K-pop channel, then turn off the TV, please."

"They won't like that," she answered without looking up. "Their fave telenovela comes on at noon."

"They can watch it later," I told her, eyeing the little yellow imps as they *eek-eek*ed in their playpen, obviously mimicking the boy band they were watching. "Wow. They're getting those moves down pat, aren't they? We might have to see if they'd like to be entered in *The Otherworld's Got Talent*."

Pixie half snorted a laugh, but said nothing when I told her to call me in case of an emergency, and I set off the seven miles to the town on the Olympic Peninsula where I had lived all my life.

I passed the turn that led out to the coast road where a big old Victorian robber baron's house sat overlooking the Strait of Juan de Fuca, and wondered what Adam was doing.

"Probably busy," I said out loud.

"I am, but only because you keep letting Pixie drive, and she is forever filling the car with french fries," a voice answered me. "Do you know how salty those are? It gets everywhere."

I glanced in the rearview mirror. "She has her license, Ako. She's allowed to drive by herself, and as unhealthy as her obsession with fries is, it's really her only food vice, so I'm inclined to see if she grows out of it."

"Bah. She could at least vacuum the front seat." The Shinigami whom I'd rescued from a local historical ghost-train tour company settled into the back seat, looking around with pleasure at the passing scenery as we left my relatively rural neighborhood and headed into town. Ako's kind were normally feared as spirits of death, but he was a devout pacifist and, when I was employed to clear him from the train, told me that he simply wanted a quiet home in a vehicle where he could sleep most of the time, and every now and again help out by keeping said vehicle tidy. It was an arrangement that for the last three months had worked out well. "Where are we going?"

"I have an appointment at the Akashic League."

His eyes grew big. "Are you—you're not—"

"I'm not sending you anywhere, Ako," I reassured him. "I told you that I would move you somewhere if you wanted, but you were welcome to stay here if you so desired."

"Whew," he said, and faded into nothing, having obviously used up his corporeal energy. I wasn't sure how much energy Shinigami could access, but the other spirits I'd known could become corporeal for a varying amount of time, depending on what type of being they were, whether they were on land considered sanctuary, or if they were wearing a powerful glamour. Only the strongest spirits could manifest in the last case, and I'd only ever seen one pull off a glamour successfully.

The rest of the drive was conducted in silence. I alternated between wondering why I hadn't heard from Adam and what I was going to do if the new head of the Akashic League insisted that I clean against my wishes.

A half hour later I was called in to meet the new head. "Karma Marx? Name's Job. Job Andrews." The man who offered me his hand looked like every other middle-aged white man: graying hair, a face that showed little expression, and a nondescript suit the color of old mud. "I expect you have a bunch of questions, am I right? Well, sit yourself down, and we'll have a little chat, you and I."

He indicated a chair as he perched on a corner of the desk, adopting a jovial attitude that for some reason gave me a case of the fidgets.

"It's nice to meet you," I said politely, glancing around the office. The decor had been changed from mildly reminiscent of an Edwardian gentleman's library, to an expensive Italian-racing-car dealership. Glossy posters depicting attractive people in sunny landscapes dotted the walls, while chrome and white leather chairs sat in a semicircle around a minimalist glass desk. "Carole had nothing but good things to say about you, and how we would be in excellent hands now that she's retired."

Job clearly didn't miss the fact that I referred to my former boss—who had been in charge of the Pacific Northwest office of the Akashic League (the Otherworld organization that controlled Summoners, necromancers, vespillos, liches, revenants, poltergeists, Alastors, and all flavors of spirits, ghosts, and ethereal beings)—because he gave me what I thought of as an ingratiating smile.

"I appreciate your concern, but I assure you that everything is going well. Very well, in fact. Now, let me see, you are a ..." He hesitated, tapping his forefinger on his temple, as if he was thinking. "Transmortis Anomaly Exterminator, yes? You banish troublesome spirits."

"That's me," I said, trying hard to quell the need to get up and move around the room. Although I was half-human, the poltergeist in me made it difficult to control the need to be moving when I was nervous.

"And you have …" He squinted at nothing in particular. "I seem to recall something being mentioned about you having run into some sort of trouble recently. …"

I forced a smile to my lips, not liking the deception he seemed to feel was necessary. It was a power play, and we both knew it. "Wergeld was bound to me when I was a child. No doubt that is what you were thinking of."

"Wergeld, yes, yes, that's it." He smiled at me, a smile that showed way too many teeth. "Although I could have sworn that the wergeld was applied more recently than … what, thirty years ago?"

"About that," I said, not wanting to talk about the tragedies of my past with him. I felt like he was smirking at me even though he kept his expression pleasant. "And yes, a second wergeld was bound six months ago."

He reached behind him and pulled out a file folder, flipping through it. "It says here that you have an unexplained ability to destroy people. The experts who examined you as a child referred to it as you 'exploding' power upon others. And evidently that trait continues to this day, since two mortals are dead by your hand." His gaze grew shrewd and very pointed. I fought to keep my fingers from twitching.

"There's been no real explanation of what happens to me when I'm attacked, no, but I've lived with my ability for more than thirty years without it harming anyone—"

"The incident earlier this year says otherwise. No." He set down the folder and rose, moving around to the back of the desk. "No, we cannot have this. We can't have loaded guns like you putting others at risk, *mortals* at risk. It will not be allowed."

"I assure you that I'm—"

He sat and spoke over me. "For that reason, I am revoking your TAE status. You are simply too dangerous to be allowed out amongst mortals while interacting with spirits. In fact, I'm going to order a monitoring device be bound to you, so that we can make sure that you are not put in a position where you can 'explode' on any other innocent mortal beings."

"I never—" I started to protest, ire riding me until I stood up to make my point.

"You will be required to wear the monitoring device—I believe we have them available in watches now—at all times. The device will report back your activities to your supervisor."

"My supervisor?" I had a hard time picking out what outrageous thing I needed to address first.

"You will be reporting to me personally," he said, pulling out another file folder, and pretended to study something in it. "Naturally, someone as volatile as you must have the highest level of supervision. Now, since you have been demoted from TAE status, you will have to help out the pest crew."

"Pest?" I repeated, disbelief momentarily depriving me of the ability to reason with him. "But that's—"

"Kobolds, imps, skrats, and boggarts, yes." Job looked over the folder at me, his once-jovial expression now tight with irritation. I wondered why he had even bothered to put on a nice first impression when he knew all along he was going to kick me down to the lowest rung of the Akashic League. "You can't get into much trouble there."

"I trained for thirteen years to be a TAE," I said after counting to eight. "I have served the League for more than twenty-five years without incident—excluding the one earlier this year, of which there were extenuating circumstances—so to punish me by kicking me down to the status of a rat catcher is not only insulting on a personal level, but idiotic. There are no other TAEs in this region of the country. I'm the only one who has the ability to deal with troubled spirits, and—"

"You are uncontrolled, violent, and irresponsible," he thundered, taking me by surprise. I stepped back, bumping up against the chair, my hands shaking with the need to control myself. "And if I had my way, I'd have you banished right now. Hear me, and hear me well, Karma Marx, if you step one foot out of line, if you forget to dot an i or cross a t, I will see to it that you find your ass tossed into the Akasha without any hope of recall. Do I make myself clear?"

"You can't do that," I protested, shocked to the tips of my toes at his threat.

What would happen to my spirits? Who would take care of gentle Cardea, goddess of my pantry, of the dada, of the imps, and Ako? What would Pixie do? She'd been through so much in her short life, and although she was as snarky as the day was long, I knew she preferred to live with me.

"I can, and I will." He looked down at his papers, his frown prodigious. "You are dismissed. Pick up your monitoring device from security before you leave. If it's not activated within twenty minutes, I will consider you in breach of your contract with the League, and will begin banishment proceedings."

I fumed silently for a few seconds before realizing it would do no good. Job had me by the short and curlies—so to speak—and there was nothing I could do. I left his office without saying a word, still shaking from the effect of the verbal attack.

"Karma?"

It took me a minute to realize someone was saying my name. A woman stood in the doorway next to me, gesturing me in while casting furtive glances toward Job's closed door.

"Er …" I hesitated, recognizing her as Lori, my former boss's secretary. "What's up?"

"You," she said, then with a *tsk* grabbed my sleeve and pulled me into her small office, peering up and down the hallway before quietly closing her door and turning to face me. "I wanted to catch you before you left. You just met Job, right?"

"If you could consider being yelled at, called uncontrolled and violent, as a meeting, then yes," I said, and, given the residual shakiness of my knees, sat when she waved me to a chair next to her desk. "I assume he inherited you when he took over from Carole?"

A spasm of distaste crossed her face as she took her seat, turning to face me. "No. I was demoted to secretary for all the management. He brought in his own assistant, a two-faced bastard named Neal. But that's neither here nor there—I didn't bring you in here for gossip. I know what Job did to you—Neal came in demanding your contract, and told me that Job was looking for grounds to break it and kick you out of the Akashic League."

"They can't do that," I said, worry gripping my gut with iron fingers. "For one thing, there are two cases of wergeld that bind me to the League. And for another … well, I haven't done anything else wrong that they could take action."

"I know that, and you know that, but Job was determined to clean house, as he called it. Obviously, that didn't work." She scooted her chair a smidgen closer, her volume dropping to that of a near whisper. "I was picking up some invoices I printed for accounting, and saw Neal shredding some notes. Normally, I wouldn't pay attention to that, but he got impatient with the shredder and jammed a whole bunch of pages in and left before it finished chewing them up. Our shredder is ancient, and it doesn't do more than three sheets, so I just happened to pull out the wad of papers that Neal was trying to get rid of."

I could picture the scene pretty well, and was confident that Lori had taken the opportunity to do a little snooping on what her new boss and his assistant were up to. "And what did you find?" I asked, skating over any comment about the ethics of reading documents that were clearly not for her eyes.

"A whole lot of information about you." She nodded when I jerked back in my seat, not expecting to hear that. "Names and dates, details of your jobs for the League, your history ... everything. And some handwritten notes about possible situations they could set up to force you to break terms of your contract."

"Why on earth does Job have it in for me?" I asked, confused.

"I have no idea. I just knew when I saw those half-shredded notes that I had to warn you. And as it happens, I have a situation that will get you out of the area for a few weeks, if you're open to that."

"I don't know what going away for a few weeks will do if Job has a target on my back," I said, my mind squirreling around with combined panic and disbelief. What had I done to bring down the wrath of the

Akashic League on my head? The situation of a few months past had been dealt with, so for Job to be picking me out for such treatment indicated a grudge on a personal level.

"Normally, I would agree, but if there's anything I've learned in the last two months of working with Job, it's that he has a very short attention span. If something—or someone—he is fixating on is out of the range of his ability to interact, then he focuses elsewhere. I think it has to do with his personality type—he has to see the results of his actions in order to receive gratification. That's why I thought of you when it came to my little project."

"What project is that?" I asked almost absently, still puzzling over why the new regional director would have it in for me.

"I have a friend named Rennie Taylor. We went to college together, and were … well, we were close. Very close." She glanced at me to see if I picked up on the inflection of the last few words.

I nodded, my mind still partially worried about what was going on with Job.

"Well, that lasted a few years after college, but then it just kind of fizzled away. You know how these things go." She made a vague gesture that I assumed was intended to convey the frivolity of some romantic relationships. "We remained friends, despite that. She always had my back when my first job … well, we won't go into that. It doesn't matter. And I had Rennie's back, which means when she met and married a man named Alan, I was supportive and happy for her. I won't say it wasn't hard seeing her fall for a man who had more money than common sense, but that's so often how life is, isn't it?"

"Absolutely," I told her, wondering now where this was going.

"Rennie took up a position with the League as a vespillo—"

"Hold up," I told her, raising my hand and already shaking my head. "I can see where this is going, and I'm afraid it's going to be impossible. Our new overlord just informed me that I am to limit myself to ridding the world of imps, kobolds, and their ilk. I can't clean anything else, let alone the spirit essences that vespillos use."

"Luckily, that's not what I need for you to do." She scooted forward a second time, making me feel a tad uneasy. "I should have said that Rennie *used* to be a vespillo. Her husband, Alan, put a stop to her practicing her art because ... well, who knows exactly what reason he gave her. I just know he's controlling, domineering, and doesn't like her having a job, especially one that concerns the Otherworld. He hates anything to do with it, which naturally means things are awkward whenever I try to see her. But that's not the worst of it. Rennie hasn't said as much, but I suspect he's abusive to her, both physically and emotionally."

"Poor woman," I said, my sympathy now engaged. "I don't know what I can do to help her personally, although I do have a friend who's a member of the Watch, and I'm sure he can take action if her husband is abusing her—"

"Alan is mortal, unfortunately, and without Rennie willing to testify against him ..." Lori let the sentence trail off with a grim twist of her lips. We both knew that the Watch was not allowed to police mortals unless their actions constituted a serious crime against a denizen of the Otherworld.

"So where do I come in?" I asked, intrigued despite my desire to run away and hide from the world. I had too many responsibilities to do that, but oh, how I wanted to.

"I want you to find Rennie. I want you to contact her and make sure she's OK. I haven't heard from her in six weeks. She's not answering her phone, texts, or emails."

"Naturally, I'll do what I can, but surely you would be in a better position to get her into a safe place? She won't know who I am even if I did get in contact."

Lori took a deep breath, her fingers white where she gripped the chair arms. "That's part of why I want someone else to look for her. Alan knows about us, about our past, and because I still work for the League, he has insisted she go no contact with me. And there are things he's doing—things Rennie hinted at before she went radio silence—that make me very worried, indeed."

"If it's something illegal, we can call in the mortal police," I told her.

"If only it was that easy. Alan is clever, so very clever. Rennie told me that just two months ago, they were in the car together, and they nearly had an accident." She leaned forward, her voice dropped to a near whisper, the intensity in it sending a little ripple of goose bumps down my arms. "He swore that he had it in his power to kill her by disabling her airbag, ensuring that he'd survive while she wouldn't. He told her that unless she stopped talking to me, he'd go through with his plan. And two weeks later, she stopped answering my attempts to reach her. Karma, I'm worried. Her husband has isolated her from everyone, and she can't get the help she needs to break away from him before he carries out his horrible threat."

"Are you sure she hasn't been harmed yet?" I asked, my fingers itching to call Adam with a demand he help.

"Yes, thankfully. Alan and Rennie were planning on taking a trip to Europe next week, and from what his travel agent says—I was supposed to go on the trip, as well, until two weeks ago when Alan had a meltdown and insisted I cancel—they are still both booked on the train and flights to France and back."

"That's reassuring, but I'm not sure what you expect me to do if they are going to be out of the country," I said slowly. "For one, I'll be here in the US, and for another, I'm not a tracker or even skilled at locating people."

"You don't need to be," Lori said, brightening, then spun around and pulled open the nearest drawer, extracting a glossy pamphlet before dropping it on my lap. "You just need to have a free seven days."

"The Byzantine Express," I read, then looked up. "She's going to be on a fancy European train?"

"Yes. It's the one featured in that movie," she said, pointing at a line on the pamphlet that talked about the train's connection to one of my favorite authors, Agatha Christie. "They normally run between Paris and Venice, but a couple of times a year, the train holds a murder-mystery event, and it goes from Paris to Istanbul. Originally, just Rennie and I were going to go, but then Alan decided I wasn't to be trusted anymore, and he insisted that he'd go, saying he loves murder dinner-theater events, and trains, and … oh, everything. Which is odd, because he never mentioned any of that before, but there we are. It doesn't sound like fun to me; I was only doing it because Rennie always had a flair for that sort of thing—she has a drama degree—but now the point is moot."

Personally, I thought it sounded like fun, but I kept my opinion to myself. "The fact remains that I'll be limited to contacting her via phone if she's in Europe, and I'm not sure how you expect me to talk to her and see if she's OK if she's not answering her phone."

"That's the brilliant thing," she said, tapping the pamphlet. "You are going to be right there on the train with her."

I may have gawked at her for a second or two—I was so surprised by that statement that I felt like my jaw sagged a little. "I *what*? Lori, much though I'd like to help you and provide support for your friend, that train trip has to cost a small fortune. Not to mention I'm sure it's booked way in advance—"

"Yes, yes, but that's all taken care of, don't you see? I used a little windfall I got from my grandmother, and splurged on an expensive suite cabin. I can't get a refund on it, and the train people say that unless I transfer ownership of the suite to someone else who will use it on that trip, then it'll just be empty. And in a way, this is better than my original plan, because Alan doesn't know you, and he won't be suspicious that you're there to help Rennie get away from him. Please, Karma, please say you'll do it. It'll help both of us—it'll save Rennie from her abusive husband, and will get you out of Job's eyeline for a while."

I won't go over the next fifteen minutes, since it consisted of me repeatedly trying to point out that I couldn't pay for such a trip, and her insisting that she didn't expect me to contribute anything toward the trip, since I was doing her a favor.

In the end, I told her I'd think about it.

"I understand your hesitation," she told me as I got to my feet, her expression filled with mingled hope and despair. "But please, please think of Rennie. She's my oldest and dearest friend, and the fact that I can't be there for her is killing me. You can do what I can't, though, and I would be eternally grateful to you if you could see your way clear to helping her."

"Let me think about it," I repeated as I opened the door and stepped out into the hallway. Job was standing with a tall, ginger-haired man, both of whom turned to look at me as I emerged from Lori's office.

"What are you doing?" Job snarled at me, his face turning red. "And why haven't you picked up your monitoring device? I see what it is you're doing—you're trying to set the staff against me. I won't have it! Insubordination is grounds for corrective action, and if you think you can get away with that sort of crap, you can think again. Neal, this is the one I told you about. Since she is clearly refusing to get fitted with the monitoring device—"

"I'm on my way right now," I interrupted, biting back a few comments of my own, but, as I turned to head down the hallway, said in an undertone to Lori, "Send me the ticket information. I may do something I regret if I stay here."

TWO

"Happy birthday, honey." My dad met me at the door when I returned home, giving me a kiss on my cheek and wrapping one of his three arms around me, escorting me into the living room before taking the two bags of groceries I held out to the kitchen.

"It's not my birthday until next week," I called after him, frowning when I noticed the TV was still on, although the imps were now seated in a row watching *Sesame Street*. I figured there were worse things for them to be doing, so didn't turn off their program, although I did give Pixie a meaningful look. She missed it, being engrossed in her phone.

Dad poked his head around the wall that separated the kitchen from the living room. "Yes, but you'll be in Europe then, so I thought I'd better say it now, before you leave."

I boggled at him, outright boggled, complete with disbelieving expression, startled eyes, and a mouth that hung ever so slightly open. "How on earth do you know about that?"

He tapped the side of his nose. "A little bird at the League told me that you accepted an unofficial job on the Byzantine Express. I'm jealous. I went on that train … oh, a good century ago … and it was delightful. I'm sure you will have a wonderful time."

"Can you transfer next month's allowance to my credit card now?" Pixie asked without looking up from her phone. "I need to order a couple of things for the trip. Matthew says it's, like, über and stuff, and I'll need a long dress for dinner because people go fancy schmancy there. There's a Morticia gown that comes in my size, and it's totally formal. Oh, and I'll need to get some more glamours, since I only have enough left for a week."

"Pixie—"

"You can't leave me behind," she said quickly, looking up to scowl at me. Behind the scowl I saw fear, which wrung my heart. She'd been through so much for someone so young, and despite her prickly personality, I'd seen the self-doubt, fear, and pain that lay beneath her protective covering. "It's against the rules. You're supposed to be there for me at all times."

"You're right," I said, coming to an instant decision. I'd taken a quick look on my phone at the email that Lori had sent, and it appeared she'd booked one of six suites available on the train, and that came with not only a double bed, but a couch that converted into its own bed. Since the suite held three occupants, I could take her for nothing more than the cost of the flights. "I'm not going to leave you behind. I'll let you have your allowance, and some of the discretionary fund that the League Home for Innocents gave me for your expenses, so go ahead and get a few outfits, extra glamours, and whatever else you need for ten days. We'll spend a couple of days at the end of the trip in Istanbul before we fly home."

She blinked a few times, having obviously expected me to argue the point, then whooped with joy and leaped up, pausing to give me a hug for a nanosecond before racing off to her room.

"Now, that's a sight to soothe even the hardest of hearts," Dad said, returning to the room. "You are a good foster mother."

"She has a point," I told him, catching sight of a flash of yellow behind one of the couch cushions. I sat down and snagged the imp that had escaped the playpen and was snoozing, plopping it with its brethren before rezipping the playpen lid. "I can't leave her alone. She's still too vulnerable. But what I want to know is, who told you about the trip? Was it Lori?"

"Can you keep a secret?" Dad asked, moving around the room to fuss with first the curtains, then the books in the bookcase.

"Of course I can. You know that."

"Well, so can I," he said with maddening calmness, flitting over to adjust a chair infinitesimally to the left, pausing to strike a pose. "You know, you could do worse than asking Adam to help you."

"Why?" I asked, wondering if I'd made a mistake to accept Lori's job. True, it wasn't employment within the standards of the League, but there was something about taking someone else's generosity that irked me.

Absently, I rubbed at the narrow black band that I wore on my left wrist. The League monitor did, in fact, resemble a lady's watch, and was calibrated, so I had been told by a serious-faced technician, to my body chemistry, which would notify Job should I use my TAE abilities. "Adam can't do anything about a mortal unless he does something heinous, like murder. And his US Marshals job doesn't have any standing in Europe, so I don't see how he could help me with the woman's husband."

Dad gave me a long look. "It's time you and he stop fighting the attraction that fills the air with static whenever you are together."

I looked away, still rubbing my wrist. "It's not like that, Dad."

"The hell it isn't. I've seen the way you two look at each other when you think the other can't see—I don't know why you can't just admit that you are meant for each other. He's a nice polter boy."

"Half-polter, and he's hardly a boy. He's a hundred and thirteen years old."

"And you're a nice polter girl."

"Again, half-polter, and a week from thirty-nine is anything but a girl."

"You like him."

"Of course I do. He's a good man. He cares about his charges, worships at the altar of justice, and ... and ..." I stopped, not wanting to put into words the skitter of awareness that prickled on my skin whenever I was around Adam. It had been slow in coming, but my father was right in that the last few times Adam and I had been together, the air was definitely charged.

"Sexy?"

I gave in to the urge and had a little eye roll. "Why do you want me matched up so badly? You can't possibly be hoping for grandchildren."

"Not necessarily, although I wouldn't object if you gave me one or two." He continued to move around the room, touching things, his polter nature keeping him moving. That, in itself was suspicious. He was only nervy like that when he was up to something. "I just want you to be happy, honey. You've been through hell the last few years, what with your murdering bastard of a husband. You deserve a good man."

"It's been less than a year," I pointed out gently, watching my father closely. I noticed he kept glancing at the front window, and a suspicion dawned in the back of my mind. "Maybe I like being a widow. Maybe I don't need another man in my life. Maybe I'm happy on my own with just Pixie and you to keep me company."

"Karma, Karma, Karma," he said in a dismissive tone, tweaking one of the curtains. "I taught you better than to lie to yourself."

"You didn't teach me squat, since I lived with Mom from the time I was six until I was eighteen," I said sternly.

"Your mother made me nervous," he claimed, waving away my comment before moving over to the other curtain to fuss with it. "She was forever telling me what I could and couldn't do. It was impossible living with her, honey, it really was. She drove me insane."

"Oddly enough, she says exactly the same thing about you," I said, frowning as now I started looking out the window.

He spun around. "Talked to her lately?"

"Last week, yes. She's dating the golf pro at the retirement community, and is quite happy. I'll tell her you were asking after her."

He snorted, then glanced at the window, feigning surprise. "Well, will you look at that?"

"What?" I scooted over to see what he was staring at, and watched as a familiar red-and-white 1962 Rambler convertible pulled into the driveway. I turned to pin my father back with a look, but he was already moving to the door to open it and call out a greeting.

Adam Dirgesinger, member of the Otherworld Watch, US marshal, and owner of a house full of spirits, entered the house bearing a huge bouquet of flowers. "Hello, Matthew. Karma, happy birthday. I don't know if you like flowers, but I'm hoping you do."

I accepted the mass of flowers he shoved in my hands, turning my gaze to my father, who was smiling broadly until he caught my eye.

"My birthday isn't until next week, Adam, but thank you for the flowers regardless. Dad, do you have something to explain—"

"Gotta run," he said, waving all his arms, and, before I could say more, dashed out the door, slamming it behind him.

Adam cocked a glossy brown eyebrow. "Do I sense something amiss? What's Matthew done now? Do you hate flowers? Are you allergic to them?" He hesitated for a second, then added, "Just don't want to see me?"

"Yes to the first, put me in a potentially embarrassing position as usual, and no to all the rest," I said, my heart lightening at the sight of him. Adam was tall, about six foot four, with shoulders broad enough that he made me feel particularly petite, and I was anything but that. But it was his pale blue eyes set against sooty-black lashes, and dark brown hair that swept back off his brow, that had started to haunt my dreams, leaving me feeling itchy and wanting. "Unfortunately, I suspect that he's right about one thing, and he will no doubt be back later to watch me eat crow. You hungry?"

"Not for crow," he said, following me into the kitchen as I got out a vase and arranged the flowers. "What's made you uncomfortable? Your visit to the League HQ?"

"You know about that, do you?" I bent to sniff at the carnations, my favorite flower.

"Matthew said you were there, and got some sort of censure, but that you were headed to Europe for a couple of weeks on a rescue mission. You want to tell me about it?"

"Yes, but …" I glanced down the hall, but Pixie's door was closed, the bass thump emerging from it indicating she was listening to music. "But first I want to ask you something. Do you … er …" I cleared my throat. "Do you think I'm attractive?"

He narrowed his eyes, sitting at the kitchen table when I indicated a chair. His gaze was too much for me, so I bustled around, turning on the electric kettle for tea and setting out some of the homemade ginger cookies that Pixie had made the day before. "What did the League director have to say to you that has you suddenly riddled with such a lack of self-confidence?"

"He has nothing to do with it. This is …" I gave a little cough. "This is personal."

His eyes widened. "Ah. You mean, do I—"

"Yes." I tried to take a pose at the sink that didn't make me look like a blob, squaring my shoulders and sucking in my stomach.

"Do I find you sexually attractive?" he asked.

I felt my face flaming, but kept my gaze on his, needing to have this out. "Yes."

"Of course."

"Oh. Good."

He pursed his lips for a second, absently toying with one of the cookies. "Are you trying to ask if I want to sleep with you?"

"Well … I guess so."

"Ah."

I waited; then he leveled both barrels of those beautiful pale blue eyes at me, just about stripping the air out of my lungs. "Yes. Do you?"

"I think so." I bit my lower lip, feeling more awkward than I ever had in my life. "I think … yes."

He gave a little nod, just as if that settled the question. "You're a lovely woman, Karma, but beyond that, you're clever, and unusually perceptive. I like both of those qualities. You told me when your husband died that you wanted some time, and I am happy to give you that if you still need more. But if you don't, then I'm more than willing to make your father the happiest man on earth."

I gawked at him for a moment before he chuckled.

"Dammit, has Dad been at you to date me again?" I asked, annoyance ridding me of the awkwardness of the moment. I poured water into my favorite teapot, and set it and two mugs on the table. I knew that Adam, like me, took his tea black, without any sweetener.

"Only every week," he said, accepting the mug I gave him, his fingers on my hand. "I won't say that I was averse to hearing his encouragement, but it's you that matters, Karma. If you aren't ready for a relationship—"

"I don't know what I'm ready for," I said, turning my hand so that I twined my fingers through his, giving them a little squeeze. "No, that sounds idiotic. I know that there is something between us that I want to investigate. I just don't know where it's going to go, so if you were hoping for something with guarantees—"

"Life doesn't give us guarantees," he interrupted, then lifted my fingers to his mouth, kissing my knuckles. "I'll settle for just the chance to see what sort of sparks we can make."

"Sparks sound good," I said, flushing again, wanting badly to fan myself with the passion that shimmered in his eyes.

"Deus, are you two going to have sex right here in the kitchen?" Pixie stomped her way into the kitchen, spreading her standard glare between Adam and me. "You have to go somewhere else to do that. Not only is it going to make me need even more therapy sessions than you already make me go to, but I want to get the butternut squash gnocchi made so it has time to chill for tomorrow, and I can't do that if you two are having sex on the table."

Adam released my hand, but I could see a smile twitching his lips.

"You have the worst timing ever, Pixie," I told my charge. "Not that Adam and I would even consider indulging in adult activities outside of a locked room. Did you get your things ordered?"

"Most. I had to pay extra to get them here by the end of the week. Is Adam coming with us?"

I glanced at the man in question, startled by the question. "Dad said something about me asking you for help, but I never thought … I mean, it is a suite, and room for three … but I didn't know …" I stopped, then asked, "Do you want to come with us? You'd have to buy your own plane tickets, because Lori is covering mine, and I am paying for Pixie, but at least the train trip itself wouldn't cost anything, and meals are included."

"It sounds like a marvelous trip, but I'm scheduled to testify in a case next week, so I'm afraid I'll have to pass."

"Watch case or mortal case?" I asked.

"Marshal case. Organized crime ringleader." He gave me a steamy look out of the corner of his eyes.

"But if I'm not going to be needed after the first day, I may take you up on the offer."

My cheeks warmed again, but I didn't want to embarrass any of us, so I kept my hands to myself, and said simply, "Consider it a standing offer if you can get away from your trial. I suppose I should go look at my closet and see what I have that's suitable to wear."

"Do you need any help?" he asked.

I blinked for a couple of seconds, a bit startled by the blatant way he indicated that he wanted into my bedroom. I glanced quickly at Pixie, unsure of how to tell him that although I was interested in moving our relationship to the next stage, I was not at all comfortable with public shows of affection in front of Pixie … including not-so-subtle innuendos.

While I was going through those thoughts, Adam pulled up his phone, flipping through a couple of screens before offering it to me. "Friend of mine has a wife who makes clothes. She has a shop in Seattle. I'm sure if you needed something for the train ride, she'd be able to hook you up."

"Oh—er—yeah, that would be great," I said, relieved. We spent another half an hour talking about the trip; then Adam stood up to leave.

I followed him out to the living room while Pixie was happily snarking back to a gnocchi-making video. "I hate to ask this of you, but can you look up information on two people for me?"

"Of course," he said, but I felt guilty under the impact of his questioning eyes.

"It's the woman who asked me to go on this trip to check on her friend. I'm a bit uneasy about it."

He pulled out his phone prefatory to accessing whatever databases he used, and cocked an eyebrow at me. "I would be more than a little concerned about someone who gave me an expensive train trip across Europe just for checking in with a friend. What are the names?"

I told him, feeling guilty that I was looking into Lori and her friend, but not wanting to take Pixie into a situation that might prove problematic. I collected up some of the imps' toys, and put them and a bowl of their favorite food—raspberries—into an oversized plastic tub. "Did you find them?" I asked, ferrying the imps into the tub before snapping down the lid onto it. I'd used a drill to punch two dozen holes into the lid but, with an eye to the way they pig piled on the bowl of raspberries, wet a towel in the bathroom and returned to the living room.

"Yes, Lori Greene, forty-three. Hmm. No criminal history. Two parking tickets seventeen years ago, but that looks like the sum total."

"What about Rennie Taylor?" I asked, taking up a stance next to the imp feasting container.

He tapped on his phone a few more times. "She's clean, as well. Nothing—" He looked up as he spoke but stopped, his eyes growing as he took in the apparently blood-splattered plastic tub. "Christ, Karma! What are they doing to each other?"

"Nothing. This is how they eat raspberries," I said, looking at the gruesome splatters of red that dripped down the walls of the container. Inside it, the imps were squeaking with absolute joy as they consumed the berries.

"It looks like the site of a slaughter," he said, giving the tub one last look before returning to his phone.

"Well, at least I am reassured that Lori isn't indulging in human trafficking or something equally heinous,"

I told him, waiting until the last of the berries had been consumed before I started plucking the imps out one by one, wiping them down with the damp towel.

"No sign of that. Let's see what the Watch can tell me. … Lori Greene, necromancer, works for the Akashic League—"

"Wait, what?" I paused in the act of wiping one of the imps, who promptly started squirming and *eek-eek*-ing at me until I placed him back in the playpen. "Lori is a necromancer?"

"That's what it says. Rennie Taylor née Watson, vespillo, was employed by the League until a year ago. No criminal history on them with the Watch, either." He gave the imps another look, watching as I absently wiped them down before returning them to the playpen.

"What's a vespillo?" Pixie asked, entering with a smear of flour on her cheek. "Raspberry day, huh? I am so not cleaning their tub."

"You know the rules—she who gives the berries cleans the tub, so yes, I will do so." I turned to Adam, asking, "Why didn't Lori tell me she used to be a necromancer? She was my boss's secretary for … oh, as long as I can remember."

He gave a half shrug. "Is there a reason why she should have?"

"What's a necromancer? Wait, is it like the video game guys?" Pixie asked.

"No," I told him, rubbing my arms. "I'm just being overly cautious. Thanks for looking that up for me, Adam."

"Anytime." He sent me a look that had me wishing I had the time for dalliance, and, with a goodbye to Pixie, took his leave.

"What—" Pixie started to ask when I went to consult clothes I hadn't worn in what seemed like an eternity.

"A necromancer is someone who can raise spirits," I told her, grimacing at my closet. "In three different forms: spirits, liches, and Alastors, although the last are very rare and hard to find. Why did I buy nothing but neutral colors for the last ten years?"

"Because your life was dull?" Pixie asked.

"Mmm." I didn't agree, but had to admit that judging by my wardrobe, I was in a funk. A bland color funk. "Vespillos, because I can feel you about to ask, are the people who find the essences that people leave behind when they pass. Usually the two work together. Does this look suitable for a fancy train trip?" I pulled out a long black dress.

"If you want to look like my grandma going to a funeral, yes. Can you do the necromancer thing?"

"No, I can't summon spirits. Only banish them."

"That's just lame. I'd like to summon them. Imagine having your own ghost army! You could make people do whatever you wanted."

"It's been tried, and failed. Spirits, as a rule, don't like to be treated like mindless drones, and the ones with corporeal abilities are even less inclined to fall into place before a power-hungry necromancer. Well, there's nothing for it. I'll have to call Adam's friend in the morning and see what she has in stock."

Pixie eyed the clothing I'd pulled out and now stuffed back into the closet. "Yeah, because your things seriously crawls my blood."

"It what?"

"Deus! You're so … like … gah!" She spun around on her heel and stalked off to the kitchen.

I did a quick Google on teen slang, and wondered if I was ever going to get the hang of having a sixteen-year-old in the house.

Three days later, Adam, Pixie, my father, and I emerged from the local bowling alley, where Pixie had demanded we go on the weekly family outing that I had instigated at the recommendation of the foster home. "I don't see why mortals are so mean," Pixie said, sniffing loudly when Dad burbled happily about beating us all. "I could have smeared Matthew all over the ground if I didn't have the glamour hiding my extra arms."

I took Adam's arm when he crooked his elbow for me, secretly delighted at the gesture. We were headed for the local Italian restaurant, and although the focus of the evening was instilling and strengthening family bonds, it felt enough like a date that Adam and I had indulged in a little discreet light flirting when the others were occupied elsewhere. "Considering you used to be mortal, that's a slightly hypocritical statement," I pointed out.

"Not to mention the fact that I put on a glamour, too," Dad pointed out, having taken the opportunity of temporarily magicking away his third arm to wear a short-sleeve shirt in the unusually warm early-summer weather. "I had the use of the same number of arms as you had. Which means I'm the better bowler. Winner has dinner bought for him, right?"

I narrowed my eyes at the look he shot over his shoulder at me, but I could tell he was teasing. "After buying clothes at Adam's friend's wife's shop—which is very nice, by the way, and thank you for telling me about it—not to mention paying for Pixie's plane ticket, and our emergency 'we need them superfast' visas to get into Turkey, I'm just about broke, so I think you can pay for your own dinner despite your prowess on the bowling field."

"Lane, not field," Dad corrected, but he was clearly pleased with the world.

We had a surprisingly nice time at dinner. Pixie, in her newfound foodie knowledge, tended to be a bit critical of other people's food, but just when I thought I'd have to quietly remind her that telling a waitress there was too much basil in the red sauce was rude (even though her complaint was valid), the harried owner came out and apologized for the new trainee cook, and whisked away Pixie's and my plates.

"I will personally make the sauce," he assured me. "I don't know what Ramone was thinking—he's my wife's sister's brother-in-law's son—but when I tasted the sauce, I knew I couldn't let you eat it."

"Can I see your kitchen?" Pixie asked. "I'm on Instagram, where I show people the things I cook, and I'd like to see what you do with your sauce."

"I'm sure that's against all sorts of health department rules—" I started to say, but the owner surprised me.

"You can't be in the kitchen, but you can stand at the service window outside it and watch me, if you like," he said, bustling away, Pixie hot on his heels.

"Well," Dad said, glancing from me to Adam. "Looks like two's company, three's a crowd. What say I take my dinner over to an empty table and leave you two lovebirds alone, hmm?"

"Dad, stop it," I told him, stabbing my fork into a bit of salad that I hadn't finished eating before our entrées arrived. "The more you try to push us together, the longer it'll take for us to actually do it."

The second I said the words, I closed my eyes at my unintentional innuendo.

Adam laughed outright, the movement causing his leg to press against mine in a way that made me very aware of his body next to me. "I'm going to assume you didn't mean that the way it came out. Oh Christ, now I'm doing it."

"I'm sorry, it's my mouth. It has always had a mind of its own and does what it wants—gah!"

Adam laughed even harder, while Dad looked amused.

"OK. That's it." I lifted my chin and shared a martyred look between Adam and my father. "I'm not saying another word lest I inadvertently say something about riding the skin train to Happy Town."

By the time Pixie returned, Adam had mopped up the tears that had streamed from his eyes due to the coughing fit, and I had stopped giggling under my breath.

"I'm going to my room now," Pixie announced when we returned home, Adam seeing us inside. My father, thankfully, had gone off to the apartment he rented above a small flower shop. "And if Adam is here in the morning—"

"You will be as polite as you always are, because you are sixteen, and you understand that what adults do in the privacy of their own rooms is no one's business," I finished for her.

"I don't suppose threatening to tell Dr. Wellbottom that you're shacking up with a man while I'm here isn't going to get me, say, another dip into money they give you for me?" she asked.

"I feel obligated to mention that blackmail is illegal in both the mortal and immortal worlds, and is very much not recommended to do in front of an officer of the law," Adam said, taking my leftovers and going into the kitchen, obviously giving me a private moment with Pixie.

Pixie glared after him. "It's going to suck having you dating a cop."

I cast her a worried look, then took her arm and hustled her down the hall to her bedroom, closing the door behind us before asking, "I'm not going to ask you if you're upset with Adam being around, because I know you like him. So now I'm wondering if you're unhappy with me. Does the thought of me having a romantic partner upset you?"

"Deus! Is that all you think about? Sex, sex, sex!" she said, shedding the glamour so that all four arms were flung into the air with a standard Pixie dramatic gesture.

I watched as she threw herself on her bed. She was always hard to read, having such a volatile range of emotions that I put down to the hard last few years she'd lived through, as well as puberty and normal teenage angst. "I wasn't aware that I was making you uncomfortable with my relationship, budding as it is, with Adam, but if it truly upsets you, then I will make sure that we behave more decorously when you are present."

"Like I'm a child?" She slapped the blanket on her bed. "You don't have to treat me like I'm some sort of an idiot, Karma. I know about sex."

That didn't surprise me. "But it makes you uncomfortable to see Adam kiss my hand? Or for us to be together?"

"No!" she answered, waving her arms around again, then rolled over and gave me her back. "Oh, just do what you want. I don't care what you guys do. It's nothing to me."

An idea clicked into place then, and I went over to sit on the foot of her bed, putting a hand on her ankle, which she promptly jerked forward. "Pixie, you remember when I went before the Watch, and the Akashic League put the second wergeld on me?"

She murmured something that sound like a yes.

"I hope that means you remember that I told the people at the Home for Innocents that I would be more than happy to have you remain with me until such time as you chose to leave. I still mean that, you know. For better or worse, we're stuck together, and no one, not Adam, or even my dad, is going to change that. Even if Adam and I decided to move in together—and I'm not looking for that, in case you were wondering—even if that happened, it wouldn't change things between us. You're still my foster kid, and I'm your foster mom, and goddess help us, we're stuck with each other. OK?"

She said something that I didn't catch because she spoke into the pillow she was clutching.

"What was that?"

She rolled over and nudged me with the tip of her shoe. "I said you'd be stupid not to move into Adam's house. It's huge, and old, and spooky, and has Jules and Anthony, and that unicorn woman who is so shy. Adam's house is perfect. *Your* house is awful."

"Thanks," I said, patting her ankle again. "I love you, too. Now, if there are no other objections, I'm going to go see if Adam is exhibiting the patience of a saint, or if he's given up on me and left."

"He's still here," she said with a twist of her lips. "He's crazy about you. If you marry him and we move into his house, can I live in the attic?"

I smiled at her, but said nothing, just left and went out to see if she was right.

Adam wasn't in the living room, but a glance out the window showed his car was still parked behind mine. I was about to call for him when he emerged from the laundry room with his arms full of imps, all of whom were making soft little moans of happiness.

"Oh lord, did they get out again? I'm so sorry. They keep chewing through the mesh sides of the playpen. I'm going to have to get them something sturdier. Here, they can go into the flour drawer for the night." I hurried into the kitchen and opened up the large drawer that had been suitably decorated for their comfort, including a gerbil water bottle, a small litter pan, and a plush cat bed.

"I hate to say this, because it makes me sound like the worst sort of narcissist, but I think that your imps have, for lack of a better expression, a crush on me." Adam attempted to deposit the imps into their night-time sanctuary, but all six of them clung to him, identical expressions of adoration on their tiny faces. Two of them gently chewed on the fabric of his shirt, their eyes filled with the imp version of devotion.

"Yeah, they're highly prone to that sort of thing. Last month it was Pixie's social worker. They clung to her legs and we had to use a rubber spatula to pry them off her when she wanted to leave. Just come over to the sink, and I'll show them the sprayer."

A horrified expression crossed his face. "You're going to spray me like a misbehaving cat? This is my favorite shirt. Nita gave it to me for Christmas."

"She has very good taste," I commented, making a note to ask her what sorts of clothing Adam liked. I knew that Amanita and he had been together in the past, but now had a purely platonic relationship that worked for both of them. "And of course I'm not going to spray you or the imps. But they don't know that, and they hate getting wet."

It took only spritzing the sink a few times and aiming the nozzle of the sprayer at the little beasts before they reluctantly allowed themselves to be tucked into bed. I gave them a small clump of grapes to get them through the night, and made sure the drawer was secured with an elastic cord before returning to the living room.

"So," I said, feeling all shades of awkward. Adam stood looking out the window at the darkness, his hands clasped behind his back.

He turned. "Get them put away for the night?"

"Yes." I cleared my throat but said nothing else, unsure of how to start things rolling. Did I just jump him? Invite him to step into my bedroom and get naked? Covertly indicate that I was up for some sexy times and hope he took the hint and initiated it? I shook my head, covering my eyes for a moment. "Oh, goddess."

"I take it that you aren't as ready to move forward as you thought," he said, his voice gentle as he moved over to stand in front of me. He didn't touch me, but I felt the heat of him as if he did. "Karma, I will never ask you to do something that you're not wholly on board doing, not that I think you would, because you're no fool, nor are you a pushover. But in case you need to hear it, I won't. If you need more time, that's fine. We can take as long as you need."

"That 'oh, goddess' was directed to me, not you," I said, uncovering my eyes. "It's because I was trying to think of a way to pass off control of the situation to you, so I don't feel like a woman desperate to get a man into bed so she can frolic all over him. Which is stupid, because if I want to do that, and you want to do that, then why am I making such a big deal about who initiates what?"

His lips twitched again.

I pointed a finger at his mouth. "Don't you dare laugh at how horribly awkward I am at this! It's been twenty years since I dated. I can barely remember what it's like."

"It's not like it's riding a bike," he said, taking hold of my hips, and gently pulling me into a loose embrace.

"Says the man who has seventy more years than me to have dated." I smiled against his mouth when he began to kiss the corners of my mouth, and put my hands on his chest after a minute of that. "Not that I want you to stop, but I'm not comfortable doing this out here. Pixie was having a bit of uncertainty as to my commitment to her with you in the picture, and while I think I reassured her that nothing will change no matter what you and I do, I'd rather not be snogging right out here until she's a bit more used to the idea."

Pale blue eyes that were hot enough to steam broccoli considered me. "Is that an invitation to your bedroom, or a very nicely phrased, if a bit indirect, request to leave?"

"Oh, I don't want you to leave," I told him, gently nipping his lower lip before I took his hand and led him to my room.

Once the door was closed (and I made sure to lock it), the awkwardness washed over me again like a bucket of cold water.

Adam stood looking at me.

I looked back at him.

"OK," he said, nodding like I'd spoken. "I see what you mean. This is a bit awkward. What would you like me to do?"

"If I said strip naked, then make sweaty bunny love to me, would you?" I couldn't stop myself from asking.

"With pleasure." His eyes never left my face, which earned him a bonus point since I kept slipping little glances to his chest, wanting badly to ogle it in its naked state. "But I think it might be better if we take this one step at a time. How about we sit on the bed and neck for a bit?"

"Neck?" I asked, laughing, but I did, in fact, sit on the bed, turning toward him when he did the same. "Boy, you really are over a hundred years old. The current term according to my recent Google dive into what sixteen-year-olds say, my ancient but sexy policeman, is sucking face."

He grimaced.

"What?" I asked, suddenly horrified that he was repulsed by the idea of foreplay.

"It's just …" He made a vague gesture before wrapping his arm around me and pulling me up close. "Earlier this week, I was called out for a case where a boggart literally sucked off the face of a mortal who had died in an alley of a drug overdose."

"Ew," I said, giving a little shiver.

"That's why the phrase is a bit too literal. For me, at least."

"No, I can see that. OK, we'll go with making out, instead."

"I am totally go with that plan," he said, and a few pleasurable minutes were spent during which he kissed me mindless.

By the time we came up for air, we were both panting, and I felt like I was a good ten degrees hotter than when we started.

"Too many clothes on," I said, pushing him backward at the same time I straddled his lap, working my way down the buttons of his shirt.

"Yes, you do have too many," he agreed, trying at the same time to peel off my shirt, his hands warm on my breasts when he managed to whip off my shirt before allowing me to lay bare his chest.

"Oooh. It's just how I imagined it would be," I said, spreading my fingers across the heavy pectoral muscles. "Would it be rude of me to say that you have just the right amount of chest hair? It's enough to make me very aware that you're a man, but not so much that I want to buy you a manscaping razor."

"No, not rude at all," he answered, pulling me down over him even as his hands were busy unclasping my bra. He had that off quickly, too, and took possession of my breasts while I was still stroking my hands lovingly over the planes of his chest and belly. He didn't have an actual six-pack, but it was close to it, and once again, I was made aware of the difference between our bodies.

"I like your chest a lot. You're all hard lines, strength, and muscle." I stopped caressing his chest for a minute, sitting upright. He took the opportunity to remove his shirt completely. I frowned at his arms.

"What's wrong?" he asked, his hands back on my breasts, which greatly enjoyed the attention.

"It's you. You're buff, Adam. Not just buff … gorgeous. Look at you! You probably never skip leg day, whereas I'm all soft and pudgy and haven't been to a gym in about twelve years."

He nuzzled the underside of one of my breasts. "You are perfect. What you think of as soft and pudgy I think of as delicious curves that sing a siren song of delight and wonder. Why the hell didn't we do this months ago?"

"Dead husband," I said, gasping when he took one nipple in his mouth, my back arching of his own accord.

"Oh, right." He repeated the action to my second breast, looking confused when I slid off his lap.

"You need to be naked," I told him, reaching for his buckle.

"I do." He beat me to it and wiggled out of his jeans and underwear, while I peeled my own pair of pants off, leaving me in my underwear.

When I turned back, I was met with the sight of a fully aroused penis standing erect and waving ever so slightly at me.

"If I said 'woof,' would you understand that was praise?" I asked, still watching it.

"I will, although I assure you that such a reaction isn't necessary."

"Yeah, well … woof!" I said, then shucked my undies and resumed my position on his lap, my knees straddling his hips. I leaned forward to kiss him again, enjoying the heat of his mouth at the same time his hands were busy on my breasts. "Do you like your nipples caressed, too?"

"Not as a rule, but you're free to try whatever you like—"

I bent down as soon as he started to speak, and lathed one little nipple with my tongue, then gently took it between my teeth.

Suddenly, I was on my back in the middle of the bed, and Adam was above me, leaning on one elbow while his mouth went wild on my breasts, his free hand stroking a path to regions south.

"I take it you are go with nipple play?" I asked with a little laugh that turned to a gasp of pleasure as his fingers found sensitive flesh.

"Yes, but not when I'm this close. Ah, you like that, do you?"

"Very much so," I said, writhing in pleasure as his fingers did a dance that had my body tensing in ever growing waves of need, want, and anticipation.

"Then I hope you'll really like this."

My eyes came close to crossing when he slid down the bed and let his tongue join the party.

I froze for a minute, my mind at war with itself. Part of me was having the best sexual experience of my life, and the other part was freaking out because … well, because I was having the best sexual experience of my life. With Adam. A man I'd only known for six months.

It was as if someone doused me with cold water. Doubt filled my brain, doubt and worry and a stupid, irrational fear that I was doing something wrong.

Adam sensed the sudden change in my response and looked up to ask, "Karma? Am I doing something you don't like?"

"No. I like it. I just …" The orgasm his touches had been building fizzled out to nothing. "I don't … dammit, I don't know what's wrong. I want this, Adam. I really want this. I like you. I like your body. My body really likes your body. It wants yours to do things to it, but …"

He moved back onto the bed next to me, one hand resting on my belly, his head propped up on his hand. "But you're not ready for this emotionally?"

"I don't know," I admitted, miserable, and feeling guilty as hell. "I thought I was. I think about you a lot, Adam. I think of things to say to you, and imagine how you'll react, and although I'm sure this makes me the smuttiest of all smutsters, I have had several really detailed fantasies involving you, a bottle of massage oil, and a horse."

"A horse?" he asked, looking more than a little startled.

"To ride. That is, you ride the horse, and I ride you." I waved away my fantasy of Adam as a Georgian highwayman, and myself as a woman traveling alone. "What's wrong with me? I was enjoying myself. I was enjoying you enjoying me."

He was silent for a moment, his eyes no longer steamy, but now bearing a thoughtful glint. "I think it's just a matter of rushing things. We have an obvious physical attraction, but sometimes, that's not enough."

"But I want a physical relationship. I want you in my life, Adam." I felt like I was about to cry with the frustration of my errant emotions.

"I feel the same, but maybe we need to take it slower. Maybe we need more time alone with each other."

I thought about that. "It's true that whenever we're together, Pixie is always with us."

"And your father. If I didn't know for a fact that he wants us to hook up, I'd suspect him of having a crush on me because he's always calling and texting me."

"He is?" I rolled onto my side so I could face him, still feeling vulnerable and as if something was wrong, but my brain worked through what he said, and it made sense.

"Yes, but admittedly, it's always in reference to you." He smiled, and I felt a little flush of warmth in my chest. "I don't mind being kept up to date with what you are doing, although I much prefer hearing about it from you rather than your father."

"We haven't had very much alone time, have we?" I said, putting my hand on his chest. He was so warm and lovely, my body wanted badly for me to seduce him, but my brain was still hesitant.

"No. How about we start dating? See how that goes before we try this again?" he asked, gesturing toward my breasts.

I gently pinched his nipple. "My breasts will always be happy to see you. And neck with you," I said, deliberately using his outdated term. "But I think you hit it—we haven't had time alone to figure out what we are together. Do you mind?"

"Taking the time to be alone with you? Not in the least."

"You are an extraordinary man, and not just because you were born with three arms, drop apports in times of stress, and can hide in shadows." I was silent for a few seconds before I kissed him. "Thank you, Adam."

"For going slow?"

"For understanding me better than I do."

"As you pointed out numerous times now, more numerous than was strictly necessary, I am older than you. Thus, I am wiser and more aware of what women need—ow!"

I giggled when he rubbed the spot on his side that I'd pinched after hearing his pompous statement.

"Do you want to spend the night?" I asked, glancing down at his erection, which was now at about half-mast.

"Just to sleep?" he asked, his eyes a bit wary.

"Yes. Unless you're opposed to a little quality cuddle time."

"I can't think of anything I'd like better, but I've had a hell of a week, and I'm likely to drop off just as you are baring your soul to me."

I scooted up until I could peel off the light blanket and sheet that I kept on my bed during the summer months. We settled into bed with me snuggled into him, his arm over me, and one of my legs tangled with his. "Considering you went to the trouble of having a woof-worthy erection for me, I will give you a pass to fall asleep while I'm indulging in pillow talk."

And that's how it was that I spent the night with the man who still filled my dreams, but now also warmed my heart with a deeper understanding of just who he was.

THREE

"There's going to be a murder-mystery game after dinner on the second night of the trip." I looked up from the papers I held when Pixie hauled herself into the kitchen the next morning, a blanket wrapped around her as she reached blindly for the French press she favored for coffee. "Lori sent me the information that the train company sent her. They've also confirmed that they switched occupancy over to us. What on earth are you doing?"

She had entered the room with one hand shading her eyes, and I assumed it was because it was almost noon, and she was up at what she referred to as an ungodly hour.

"I don't want to see the 'I've banged Adam all night' expression that you're wearing. It's too early for that."

"The only expression I'm wearing is one wondering why I'm spending so much money to make sure that you're coming with me on a trip of a lifetime. Adam is long gone, Pixie. You can safely uncover your eyes."

I didn't tell her that he'd left almost six hours earlier, after having received a call that he was needed to escort a prisoner to San Francisco, which meant he'd be out of the area for the next few days.

She slowly dropped her hand before turning to squint at me.

I stroked my hands down my hips, and said, "Oooh, baby."

"Karma!" Her shriek was enough to wake up the imps from where they were having their nap in the morning sun, and led to Cardea, the goddess spirit of domiciles who resided in my walk-in pantry, opening the door to peer out worriedly.

"Sorry," I told Pixie. "I couldn't resist. No, Cardea, nothing is amiss other than me teasing Pixie a bit. Would you like to come out to join us for lunch?"

Her eyes widened as she looked from me to Pixie, all the while backing into the pantry. "Oh. That's … oh. Such a lovely invitation, but I promised myself that I'd tackle your soups today. It's so important to have them in just the right order, don't you think?"

"I do," I said, aware that her extreme case of agoraphobia made it hard for her to leave her safe space. "Would you like me to get you a few more? I saw some new brands the other day that I thought you might like to include in the collection."

"That would be wonderful, thank you," she said, brightening. "I'll just get to work so they're ready for the new inclusions."

"I'll have my father give them to you next week. You remember that Pixie and I will be gone for about ten days, yes?"

"I do. Matthew will be taking care of us and the house," she said, nodding and quietly closing the door.

"You think she's ever going to come out of there?" Pixie asked, giving the pantry door a long look.

"Possibly. She seems to be enjoying the Zoom therapy sessions, so perhaps one day she'll feel comfortable enough to join us in the rest of the house. Now, do you want to be Mary, the downtrodden personal maid to Lady Waverly, or Amelia DeVere, dashing lady archaeologist?"

She stared unblinking at me for ten seconds.

"Right," I said, handing over the couple of sheets of paper that I'd paper-clipped together. "You can be Amelia, and I'll be the pitiable Mary. That is your character information, and no, I didn't read any of it. Just printed it and clipped together the pertinent pages."

She had taken the pages and, after making a cup of strong coffee, sat at the table, still clutching the blanket. "This says we are welcome to wear a costume appropriate to our character if we want to. Can I get one?"

"A lady archaeologist costume? There's not a lot of time for that," I warned her. "But I suppose if you find something not terribly extravagant, we could swing it. What do you think poor lady's maid Mary wears?"

"Drab, shapeless black dress," Pixie answered, pulling out her phone. "Limp, greasy hair. Maybe even glasses, and a wart or two on her face."

"Well, that paints a delightful picture," I said, sighing and pulling out my own phone. I'd bought a few dresses that served the purpose of evening wear, as well as a couple of outfits that I thought of as business casual, since the train literature made it clear that jeans were not welcome on their august carriages.

Five days later, Pixie and I entered our hotel room in Paris, Pixie full of her version of excitement, and me jet-lagged and exhausted. We dumped our luggage, and I collapsed onto one of the two beds, wishing that the world would go away and let me sleep for a day or two.

"So this is Paris," Pixie said, standing at the window for a second before she began to flit around the room. I knew it was the excitement of the trip that was making her polter fidgets come out, but had hoped the drug she'd taken prior to the flight would keep her calm for a bit longer. Evidently it had worn off, because she was almost a blur as she zipped around the room, examining and touching everything, dashing into the bathroom only to emerge with various sample sundries that had been left for us, and, finally, fussing with her luggage, taking out each item and checking it over. "It's not what I expected. It's a lot more grimy, isn't it? And loud. It's so loud. Wow, did you see this? There's actually good-quality shampoo and conditioner in here, although it doesn't say it's cruelty-free. Do you want it? I don't normally use this sort of stuff, but I read about a couple of girls from the Home talking about it, and I'm kind of curious. There's a second toilet. Why do they have two toilets in one room? Also the showerhead is huge. Like the size of a sunflower. Hey, there's a van outside that's smoking. Do you think it's going to blow up? Is it a bombing? Paris has bombings, right? Are we going to die?"

I stood it for as long as I could, then sat up and pulled my bag from where it was still strung across my chest, pulling out a small bottle of pills and holding it up for her. "Do you want to take one of the meds that Dr. Wellbottom gave you?"

"Deus, Karma!" she said, slapping her legs with all four arms before making another blur-lap around the room. "You're making me seem like a freak!"

"You're not a freak, but you are a full polter, and one who is in an exciting new place about to start an equally exciting vacation. It's normal for polters to be wired in either situation, but there's no way we can go out in public with you flickering like that. If you don't want to take the meds, that's fine, although Dr. Wellbottom said it would help out in situations like the plane ride where you need to keep from moving around a lot. We can stay in if you would prefer."

"Fine, I'll take the meds," she said with great drama, shaking out a pill before running to the bathroom to take it with a bit of water. "But if it makes me so drugged out that I can't experience everything cool, then I'll tell Dr. Wellbottom you're abusing your authority."

"I am not forcing you to do anything; I simply thought you might feel better if you weren't having to keep your polter traits in check while we're in public. The choice is yours. If you have to use the toilet, make sure you use the bigger one." I lay back down, feeling my body sink into the mattress. It was heaven. "The other one is a bidet."

"What's that?" she asked, emerging again from the bathroom.

"You wash your privates with it."

The look on her face was priceless, but I didn't have long to enjoy it before she slammed the door, and I heard the gurgle of water, accompanied by stifled giggles.

A half hour later we emerged from the hotel, Pixie calmed down enough that she just looked like an exuberant teen, and me jet-lagged to the point where I was almost numb.

"Right," I said when we reached the sidewalk, pulling out a small guidebook I'd purchased in the hotel shop. "We have three hours before we're due at the meet and greet. What sights do you want to see in that time?"

"G&T," she said, grabbing my arm and hauling me down the sidewalk toward a metro entrance.

"Is that a museum?" I asked, stifling a yawn that seemed to suck in half the oxygen available on the block. "If so, that's all we can see, since most museums take hours."

"No, it's a club. It's *the* club." She shot me a scathing look. "Everyone in the Home group was saying to go to Goety and Theurgy because anyone who's anyone in the Otherworld shows up there."

"Home ... oh, your Home for Innocents WhatsApp group?" I frowned as I tried to prod my brain cells into functioning despite their desperate demand to go immediately to bed. "I'm not sure a nightclub is somewhere I should be taking you."

"I'm sixteen, Karma!" She paused at a ticket machine, read it carefully, then inserted a few euros. "It's legal to drink here. Besides, there are all sorts of people there, important people like the Venediger."

"The what, now?" I followed her through the turnstiles and out onto a metro platform, waiting for the train. I gave up trying to be the reasonable one, and decided that since Pixie was so determined—and, more important, was taking initiative, which I felt was a promising sign—I'd go with the flow.

"Venediger. It's some woman who's the head of all the peeps in Europe. Otherworld peeps," she explained in the same tone she used when describing the steps needed to take in a recipe.

I didn't for the world want to crush this blossoming newfound confidence, so I let her chatter on for the next twenty minutes while we rode out to a somewhat bohemian arrondissement where the club was located. When we arrived at the club, I was relieved to see that it wasn't the dark, smoky hole-in-the-wall that I imagined, but a well-lit cross between a restaurant and a bar.

It was, indeed, filled with a variety of individuals, including two spirits who were dancing on a small dance floor.

"We can get something to drink and an appetizer if you like, but I don't want to take more than a little edge off the dinner we're having with the train people tonight," I told her as she claimed a small table just big enough for two, and looked around with mingled avidity and studied nonchalance.

"OK. I'll have an absinthe," she said with a little toss of her head that I figured she'd practiced.

"Will you, indeed. Oh, hello."

A waitress wandered over, eyed first Pixie, then me. "Welcome to G&T. You will read the rules, please. They are in English on the behind," she said in a heavy French accent, handing me a small paper menu.

"Rules? Is there an age limit?" I asked, glancing worriedly at Pixie. She seemed so excited about coming here, I hated to ruin her fun right out of the gate.

"The rules, please. You must read." The waitress nudged my hand holding the menu.

"Sure. Er ..." I flipped the menu over, and read aloud, "'G&T is a neutral ground. Please follow the rules: no summoning minions of any form, persuasion, or origin. No wards are to be drawn within the club, either protective or otherwise. Glamours are strictly prohibited. No exceptions will be allowed.'"

"Deus!" Pixie said, and, with an exasperated roll of her eyes, dropped her glamour.

"'Patrons who squash imps will please scrape up the mess and deposit the remains in the imp bucket.'" I stared at the waitress, my skin all but crawling. "You kill your imps here? That's horrible! I can understand about making people remove their glamours—although those aren't cheap, and I would be very annoyed if my ward here had to go out in public without one because you made her dismiss the glamour she'd just applied—but to kill little imps is just cruel."

"Yeah. They're, like, totally cool once you get to know them," Pixie said, a pugnacious set to her jaw that I had a feeling I was also close to exhibiting. "Look at what they made Karma for her birthday."

She pulled out her phone and flipped through a few pictures before she held up one for the waitress. The imps had made a heart mosaic out of tissues that they had chewed and spat onto a board, beneath which Pixie had written "Happy Birthday, Karma."

The waitress made one of those *tch*ing noises that only the French seem to make, then said, "But those are not European imps. Those are Australian, yes? They are much different. The imps here, they are trouble. They cause fires. They are cruel. It is the way of things, you know?"

"Yes, I know they are much different than my imps, but it still seems rude."

"You must finish," she said, nodding toward the menu.

"Eh? Oh. Er … 'Beings and entities who disregard the rules will be summarily dealt with by the Venediger.'" I looked up at her. She seemed to be waiting for something. "We agree to the rules?"

"*Bon,*" she said, then moved off to the table next to us.

"This place is weird," Pixie said with satisfaction, rubbing all four of her arms as she looked around. "Do you think they really kill imps? It's so mean. Ooooh, look at that person. He has horns."

"No pointing," I said in an undertone. "It's rude and we don't know how the people here take being noticed."

I pretended to drop the menu so I could bend down and cast a glance behind me.

Sure enough, one of the men at the bar had a pair of curly horns coming off his forehead. He stood next to a man with red hair and a face full of freckles, who was talking with an intensity that was clear even ten yards away. Beyond them, a woman in brown turned away and moved into the back area, where I assumed the bathrooms were located.

"That's a satyr, and you will please stay away from him. They tend to be a bit pushy when it comes to women," I told Pixie softly, before straightening up when the waitress returned for our order. "Hi again. Can we get two glasses of house white, please?"

"I want an absinthe," Pixie protested when the waitress headed to the U-shaped bar in the middle of the room.

"I know you do, but I also looked up the drinking laws in the countries we will be in, and it says sixteen is legal if accompanied by an adult. I'm not averse to you having the occasional glass of wine while we're here, but anything stronger will need to wait until you're older, OK?"

"You treat me like I'm a child," she started to say, but stopped herself before she could go into a full-fledged rant. "Fine, but I get to have champagne on the train."

"One glass a day, and only in the evening," I told her.

"Why in the evening?"

"Because I don't want it interfering with the meds you take in the morning. Do you like white wine? If you would prefer red, I will get you a glass of that instead."

"No, it's OK," she said, adopting what I assumed was her world-weary persona. When the waitress brought our glasses, along with a cheese plate that I'd ordered to soak up the alcohol, Pixie asked her, "We're from the US and we don't know anyone in Paris. Is there anyone here who is, you know, like famous?"

The waitress looked momentarily startled but, after a moment's thought, half turned and nodded toward the other side of the room, just beyond the small dance floor. "The green wyvern and his mate are in town. She is a famous demon lord and a Guardian."

Pixie and I exchanged looks. We had both met a Guardian, and frankly, I did not care to repeat the experience.

"But do not bother them," the waitress continued. "It is most dangerous, you know?"

"Wyvern?" Pixie asked, a little frown between her brows.

"Dragon," the waitress said, then hurried off when someone called for her.

"Dragons? There are dragons here?" Pixie half rose out of her chair until she remembered her woman-of-the-world persona. "Are they, like, huge with tails and things? Do you see one? I really want to see one. Do you think they'd let me take a picture?"

I shrugged. "I've never met one, but I've heard of them, and from what I've been told, they look like anyone else."

"Really?" Her nose scrunched up in disappointment. "Why would they do that?"

I nodded toward her extra arms. "If you had to go out in public looking like a big stompy dragon, or a person, which would you prefer?"

"Oh. Yeah." She glanced over at the other side of the bar again. A second set of music—which had stopped shortly after we had arrived—just began, and a few people moved out to the dance floor to indulge themselves. "I really want to see them, though."

I took a sip of the wine. "Mmm. Very nice. Light, but with a little fruity head to it."

"What is—" Pixie turned back to me, and realized she'd been missing out on her first drink. She took a big swig of it, coughed a couple of times, then said in a voice that resembled a croak. "Yeah, smooth. Come on, let's go dance."

"Pixie—" I started to protest, but she'd already leaped to her feet and started toward the dance floor.

I was about to cling to my chair and let her go dance by herself while she satisfied her need to see dragons in person, but one of the satyrs turned his head and watched her. That was enough for me. I stood up, made sure he caught the warning look I sent him, and marched resolutely after my ward.

"Which one do you think is the dragon? I don't want to meet the Guardian, because once was enough, but I really want to see a dragon and get a selfie with him." Pixie bopped regardless of the beat of the music, her gaze busy scanning the people sitting in the booths that lined that side of the club.

"I assume the dragon is the one sitting with the woman in the corner booth," I said softly. "Since she's the only woman over here."

"Oooh. Yeah." Pixie grabbed my arms and forcibly danced us toward the corner, shooting interested glances toward the people at the table. It contained a dark-haired man, a woman with curly brown hair, and a slim young man with what I thought of as a 1970s porn mustache. "Hey, if I turned so my back was to them, could you take a picture of me and get them in the background?"

"No," I told her, amused despite myself. Pixie hadn't been so excited about anything since she'd discovered blue corn. "But if you really want to meet them, you could probably introduce yourself so long as you were polite, and didn't bother them if they make it clear they would prefer to be left alone."

"Yes!" she said, and whirled around, grabbing my wrist to drag me after her as she made a beeline for the corner booth.

"—have not had much trouble now that the situation with red dragons has been …" The slim young man who had been speaking with an Italian accent paused at the approach of Pixie, his eyes narrowing on her.

"Hi," she said, holding out her hand to the man, since he was the nearest. "I'm Pixie. Karma and I are from the US. We're here for the Byzantine Express to Istanbul. Are you a dragon?"

The young man's eyes narrowed farther. "I am not. I am Cosmo Zen. I am the new Venediger, and you were *not* invited to be a part of this conversation."

"My apologies," I said, wrapping an arm around Pixie, and pulling her back slightly. "I told her it was OK to introduce herself, but I see you all are busy."

"Not at all," the woman said, obviously amused. She reached across the table to shake Pixie's hand, and said, "I'm Aisling Grey. Er … I'm sorry if this sounds rude, but which hand do you use to shake with?"

"Top one," Pixie said, shaking her hand after a moment's hesitation. "It's the arm that doesn't drop off. You're a Guardian? We met a Guardian earlier when Karma's husband died. She was mean. She helped killed Karma's domovoi, Sergei."

The Guardian Aisling looked at me with wide eyes. "What's a domovoi? Not that it matters if someone killed him. I can't believe a Guardian would do that. We have a code of standards to adhere to. Oh, this is Drake. He's the dragon."

The man stood up, and made one of those old-fashioned bows that look silly on many mortals, but which people of the Otherworld manage to pull off without looking affected. "Drake Vireo, madam," he said, shaking my hand.

"Karma Marx," I murmured.

"If you will excuse me, I have much work to do," the Venediger said, shooting me a look that had me straightening my shoulders.

"Can I get a selfie with you?" Pixie asked the green-eyed dragon. He was handsome, but I preferred blue eyes to green … and suddenly, I was hit with a wave of longing for Adam. We hadn't had time since our ill-fated attempt at lovemaking to do more than chat on the phone, and I missed him more than I expected.

Surprise flashed across his face for a second, but Aisling smiled broadly and told Pixie, "Go right ahead. He's disgustingly handsome, isn't he? He also loves to dance, and I bet if you asked him, he'd trip the light fantastic with you for a few minutes while I talk to your … er …"

"Foster mother," I said, and cast a worried look over at the dragon. He wore a bit of a martyred expression but, after allowing Pixie to take a couple of selfies with him, escorted her onto the dance floor, where he clasped her in a very Catholic-school version of a dance position, with approximately two feet of distance between them.

"I hope I didn't just piss off your husband as well as the Venediger," I said, sliding into the booth when Aisling indicated I should do so.

"Not at all to either. Cosmo is new, so he's a bit overly conscientious, but he's not bad underneath it all. And Drake and I have three kids, two of whom are daughters, so it's good for him to get used to what their teen years are going to be like. I assume Pixie is a teen?"

"Sixteen, yes," I said with a bit of a sigh, and allowed myself to sink back into the cushions. "Sometimes I wonder if I was ever that much trouble, and then she'll go and do something that just makes me want to fight the world to keep her safe."

"Spoken like a true mother," Aisling said, nodding. "Now, tell me about this bad Guardian."

I hesitated but, after a few seconds' thought, gave her a fairly bare-bones explanation of the situation surrounding the death of my husband.

"Thank you for telling me." Her expression was a bit grim. "I wish I could say such things were isolated situations, but these days … well, you know. The Otherworld is a bit topsy-turvy. So, what do you do for the Akashic League? I don't often get to talk to members of it."

"I'm a Transmortis Anomaly Exterminator," I said, then made a face. "Or I was before I was put on the back burner for a bit."

"You do something to … ghosts?" Aisling asked.

"I clean houses, yes. Or in other words, move troublesome spirits and related beings to the Akasha."

"Ouch," she said, then immediately looked contrite. "Sorry, that was rude. It's just that the Akasha is a bad place."

"It is, which is why I'm not a very good TAE. I tend to rehome those spirits who aren't causing any problems, and only banish the beings that harm others."

"Gotcha," she said, nodding, glancing over at the dance floor, where Pixie was clearly talking Drake's ear off as they moved to a slower tune. "I've only met a couple of bad spirits, although Cosmo was saying that he was having problems with one earlier today. She was here again this evening, and he was keeping an eye on her in case she got out of hand. Maybe we should tell him you're available if needed."

"I'm afraid I couldn't help him even if I wanted. My boss has decided that I need to focus my abilities elsewhere, and unfortunately"—I lifted my wrist to show the black monitor watch—"they'll know if I do anything else."

"That's a shame. Maybe—"

Pixie and Drake arrived back at the table then, and judging by the look the latter was giving his wife, I decided we'd taken up enough of their time and, after thanking them both for indulging us, took Pixie back to our own table.

"Drake says he can breathe fire, and Aisling can control it. Also, she has her own personal demon in the form of a really big black dog." She looked wistful at the last words.

"We have imps, a dada, and an agoraphobic spirit," I pointed out to her. "We do not need a demon, dog-shaped or otherwise."

"You just have no scope," she said with another stab at her world-weary attitude, tossing back the rest of her wine.

I sipped mine while she chattered away, both of us watching the denizens of the Paris Otherworld as they mingled, chatted, danced, and in a few cases got a bit too affectionate for a public place. As we were leaving, I stood waiting while Pixie went to the ladies' room to reapply her glamour. I was scrolling through messages on my phone, noting sadly that there was nothing from

Adam other than a wish that we have a smooth flight, when I was bumped from behind.

I spun around to find the redheaded man with freckles. He had stumbled over someone's bag that was protruding into the aisle. "Pardon me," he said in bad French. "Did I harm you?"

"Not at all," I answered in English, seeing Pixie emerge.

The man nodded, murmured another brief apology, and hurried off.

"Dinner in an hour," I said once we had returned to the hotel, melting onto the bed while praying for the strength to get through a couple of hours more before I could get some much-needed sleep.

"Would you mind if we didn't go?" Pixie asked.

I rolled over to look at where she sat on the bed. "No, I wouldn't mind, but I thought you were excited about seeing everything."

"Eh. They're just mortals," she said, waggling her hand. "Mortals always make me nervous. Besides, I'll have to have a glamour on so much for the next week, it'll be nice to have it off for tonight."

"It's fine with me so long as you're sure."

"We can order room service," she said, snatching up the menu. "And get champagne."

"No champagne." I lay back on the bed, the last twenty-four hours swirling in my brain. "Not until we're on the train."

That dictate didn't go down well, but after the minimum amount of time spent telling me just how much of a trial her life was, she settled down, and I was finally able to crawl into bed around eight p.m.

"Tomorrow is going to be awesome," Pixie said when I snapped off the bedside light.

"Because the trip will start?"

"Because I'm going to wear my archaeologist outfit."

"I'm not sure if the train company wants its customers in costume outside of the murder dinner event," I said slowly, sleep starting to claim me.

"They said we can't dress like slobs, or wear jeans. They said nothing about an authentic pair of lady's jodhpurs and matching coat that cost me three months' allowance," she answered, her voice rich with satisfaction. "I can't wait! It's going to be the best train ride ever. No one will be able to forget how awesome we'll be!"

I had a horrible presentiment that we were both going to regret that statement.

FOUR

"It will be my extreme pleasure to attend to your every need while you are here on the Byzantine Express. As you can see, this seating area converts to a bed for the signorina, while the doors on the main bedroom can be closed for privacy, or folded back for conversation, as they are now."

We looked at the doors to which he was gesturing. They were done with breathtaking opulence in the form of an intricate inlaid mosaic.

"The en suite is marble—Italian, naturally—and in it you will find complimentary bathrobes and slippers. The table over here allows you to have private dining if you desire. I believe you chose the first seating for meals taken outside of the suite, yes?"

"That's right," I said, doing a small 360-degree turn to take in the opulence of the Grand Suite Constantinople, as our temporary home away from home was named. It was beyond gorgeous, all gleaming glossy wood, ornate marquetry, highly polished brass, glittering crystal, and exquisite silk. I couldn't even begin to imagine how much the suite had cost Lori, and immediately felt guilty at taking such an expensive vacation.

I'd just have to see to it that I saved her friend no matter what obstacles the abusive husband posed.

"Just so. You will alert me if you desire instead to dine in your suite," Paolo continued.

Pixie stood transfixed in the center of the compartment, which was divided into three areas: a bedroom with a bed that took up almost the entire width of the cabin, a lounge area with two deep-green chairs and a matching green-and-cream sofa, all bearing hand-embroidered cushions in silk, and a bathroom furnished with a handblown tulip sink and a marble shower.

Paolo gestured toward the table. "Champagne is available at any time. There are four call buttons. Allow me to show you the locations."

We noted the position of the buttons, agreed that a little light breakfast would be acceptable, and as soon as Paolo left the suite, softly closing the door behind him, both collapsed down onto the sofa.

"Wow," Pixie said at last, taking copious pictures with her phone.

"You can say that again. Would you think I was being out of line if I forbid you to touch anything but the furniture?"

"Normally, I'd say yes, but I'm afraid that the train people will have me beheaded if I break something," she answered, getting up to examine a mirrored brass wall rack containing gold vases with flowers, two empty lead crystal decanters, and four matching tumblers. "I wonder if they have absinthe?"

"No absinthe. And remember, only one glass of champagne." I shook off the stunned sensation of being in way over my head, and moved into the bedroom to unpack the garment bag that we had each been allowed to bring into the carriage itself, being told that if we desired our larger luggage pieces, they would be brought to us as needed.

"I'm going to change," Pixie told me, then disappeared into the bathroom with her bag.

I hurried out of the clothing I had donned that morning feeling it was perfectly suitable to riding on a train, and put on my second-best outfit, a linen tunic and palazzo pants that I had planned to wear at one of the evening events. Judging by the people we'd seen getting onto the train earlier, I was going to be wearing my one good evening dress every night.

By the time I opened the doors to my bedroom, Paolo was chatting with Pixie, now clad in a belted, thigh-length sand-colored coat, matching jodhpurs, and knee-high brown boots. But it was her hair that had me stopping dead in my tracks—instead of her long black hair that she normally wore in a messy bun, she now sported a smooth black 1920s flapper bob. It had to be a wig, and yet, I couldn't figure out where all her hair went to leave the bob lying so flat against her head.

And then I caught sight of the champagne flute she held, sipping it with a nonchalant expression. "It's a tolerable vintage," she said, waving her free hand. "Mischievous but not too audacious. I like it."

"Thank you, Paolo," I said when he handed me a glass, and after asking if there was anything else we'd like, he departed.

I looked at Pixie as I took the deep armchair across the beautiful inlaid table from her. It was now covered in a pristine white cloth, with two plates laden with food, a basket of croissants and breads, several small pots containing butter and jams, and two silver teapots and bone china cups. The champagne bottle sat in its position of glory in a standing ice bucket. "Mischievous?" I asked, fighting to keep from laughing. "Audacious?"

A little giggle slipped out before she could school her face into one of indifference. She waved her hand again as she took another sip, then wrinkled her nose and hurriedly set down the flute. "Is champagne always that bitter?"

I took a sip. "It's a bit dry, but I don't see anything wrong with it."

She struggled for a minute before she said, "Do you think they have Coke here? Or something that's not quite so nasty?"

"We can ask, but for all that's good and green in the world, do not refer to the champagne as nasty. They'll likely boot us off the train if they hear that." I looked down at the plate of food: eggs, salmon, and what appeared to be caviar. "Time to up our standards, Pixie. At least temporarily."

She eyed the plate critically, and while we ate, I was treated to a running commentary about what she found offensive (mostly the champagne) and tolerable (the food, which I notice she ate with gusto, even the caviar, which I passed on). We spent a little more time prowling around the extravagant compartment until the train set off.

"What are you going to do about finding your mark?" Pixie asked, using her phone like a mirror to check her teeth for stray bits of breakfast.

"This isn't a con, kiddo. Since we have hours until lunch, I thought I'd go hang around the lounge car and see if Lori's friend and her husband go there. If they don't, then I'll watch for them at lunch."

"And then what?" she asked, patting her bob.

I watched her with fascination. "Then I'll be extremely sociable and chitchat up a storm. When did you find time to acquire such a good-fitting wig? I can't even see where you've stashed all your real hair."

"I had a couple special glamours made up with this hair," she said, giving her head a little toss. "I thought it looked more lady archaeologist. What do you want me to do?"

I hesitated, torn between not wanting her to get involved in an unsavory and potentially dangerous domestic situation and knowing full well that she would worm her way in if I didn't find a role for her. "It would be helpful to know when the husband goes into the public carriages. A log of the times he arrives and leaves would give us a chance to establish when Rennie might be safely approached if he's busy elsewhere."

"Oooh," she said, her eyes lighting up. "Undercover detective work. I like it. I can use my dig notebook."

I nodded when she pulled out an old-fashioned brown blank notebook. "Just don't get in his way or otherwise bother him. Or let him know you're watching him. Remember that he's emotionally and physically abusive to his wife, and that sort of person doesn't hesitate in striking out at others. So if you feel at all threatened, either go to one of the train attendants or come back here and tell Paolo to find me, OK?"

"Meh," she said with a one-shoulder shrug. "I'm a polter. No one can hide like me. He won't even see me watching him."

"Hiding requires shadows, and the compartments are bound to be well lit at night. Just remember that your safety is the most important thing."

With some reluctance, she agreed to be careful and not take any chances.

The bar car/lounge of the Byzantine Express was another showstopper, one that caused me to pause in the doorway to admire the entire carriage.

Windows ran the length, while gorgeous art deco wall sconces graced every few feet of wall between sapphire velvet curtains. Blue-and-white patterned love seats, and individual seats with accompanying footstools, were accented with small parquet tables. At the far end was a gleaming bar and a grand piano. The rise and fall of conversation struck us as we entered, the lounge half-filled with excited tourists pointing at sights of the French countryside as we zipped along toward Switzerland.

"I'm going to park here," Pixie said sotto voce as she plunked down the oversized brown rucksack she had informed me would be just what a lady archaeologist carried, and claimed a seat that looked down the length of the car. "What does the target look like?"

"I don't know, and stop referring to Rennie as a target. She's in need of our help, a fact you will please keep in mind. I'm going to go mingle. Let me know if you find her."

"Your friend didn't give you a picture?"

"She sent one, but it was pixelated and hard to see beyond the fact that the woman had shoulder-length brown hair. Just keep your eyes peeled, and your head down."

She rolled her eyes in obvious exasperation, but settled in with a couple of books and her notebook.

It took me almost twenty minutes to chat my way down the car, even half-empty as it was. I'm sure I startled a number of people by joining them in brief conversation, but I couldn't think of any other way of identifying who was who.

By the time I reached the three people at the grand piano, my normally introvert self was exhausted, and I desperately wanted a nap. But instead, I moved next to a portly black man and tossed out my conversational bait that I'd used the length of the car. "Goodness, we seem to be going so fast. Do you have any idea what our speed is?"

The man turned around and I could see he wore the collar of a religious man, although judging by the gray of his shirt and jacket, I assumed he was not a priest. "I'm afraid I don't, no, but we can ask one of the stewards." He offered his hand. "I'm Reverend Billie Wall, but you can call me Rev. Everyone does."

"Karma Marx," I said, shaking his hand. He had a British accent, so I took him for an Anglican vicar.

"It's a pleasure to meet you," he said. "You weren't at the dinner last night?"

"No, we were a bit tired. We had a long flight."

"You are here with your husband?" Rev asked, gentle inquiry in his eyes.

"My foster daughter. I'm a widow."

He murmured a platitude, then moved to the side to gesture to his right. "You're American? This is one of your compatriots, then. Mr. Alan Taylor, Ms. Karma Marx."

I blinked for a moment at the sight of the red-haired, heavily freckled man whom I'd last seen at G&T. He didn't seem to recognize me, though, and gave my hand a perfunctory shake before returning to the drink he was holding.

Alan Taylor? This was the man who abused his wife? I had a distinct memory of Lori telling me how he disliked anything Otherworld, and yet the night before, he was in an Otherworld bar, drinking with an

Otherworld denizen. I was curious as to why, but now was clearly not the time to ask.

I shook away my mental fog, and smiled brightly. "There seem to be a lot of us Americans on this trip. Are you traveling together?" I knew they weren't, but it seemed like the most benign way to get at the info I wanted.

"Us? Oh no. I'm here due to a bequest of a very generous parishioner," Rev said with a broad smile. "He loved this train, you see, and wanted to take one last trip on it, but sadly, was called to other pastures before he could do so. You can imagine my surprise when he left me the ticket he'd purchased for this trip. We shared a love of murder mysteries, you see, and he knew I'd enjoy participating in one on such a famous train."

"My foster daughter is excited about it, as well," I said, nodding toward the other end of the train, where Pixie was currently gazing out of the window. "That's her in the guise of an adventuring lady archaeologist. What about you, Mr. Taylor?"

"Hmm?" Alan Taylor looked up from where he'd obviously been deep in thought. "What about me?"

"Are you a murder-mystery lover, as well?"

"Yes," he said curtly, then frowned and set his glass onto the bar.

"And you're here by yourself?" I asked, aware that I was being a stereotypical obnoxiously prying American, but figuring that asking point-blank might save me some time.

He gave me an odd look out of the corner of one eye. "Who did you say you were?"

"Karma Marx. I'm here with my foster daughter, Pixie." I kept a pleasant smile on my face even though I wanted to tell him to pay attention.

"Ah." He didn't answer; before I could say more, he turned and marched out of the carriage.

Rev and I exchanged glances, but before I could say anything, he was greeted by an older couple who had just entered the lounge.

I turned back to look down the long length of the carriage, my attention immediately caught by a woman in brown who stood just beyond Pixie, her eyes fixed on the door through which Alan had just left. The expression on her face was so distraught that I murmured, "Bingo," under my breath before making a beeline for her.

She slipped out the door before I could reach her, but I hurried out with only a warning glance cast at Pixie, almost immediately bumping into the woman as she stood next to the carriage attendant's seat, which was located at one end of each of the sleeping cars.

"Oh, excuse me," I said when I almost ran her down. She had been looking out of the window as the scenery blurred by us, but the expression in her eyes when she turned to me was so gripping, I stopped trying to summon up polite chat to say, "Are you OK?"

"Yes, of course," she replied in a breathy voice, her hands clasping each other so tightly that her knuckles were white. "I'm fine. Just fine."

"You wouldn't happen to be Rennie Taylor, would you?" Her eyes widened at my words, so I hurried on. "A friend at my job told me to keep an eye out for you. I'm Karma Marx, by the way. She said that she thought you would be taking this trip, and that you might ... er ... might need a friend."

"Lori," the woman said with a near sob, then seemed to get a grip on her emotions, because the next words came out much more controlled. "Yes, I am Rennie. It's very sweet of you to be concerned, but there's no need for it. I'm … my husband …"

"I've heard about your husband," I said softly. "And I'm happy to help in any way I can."

Her eyes, a near solid black, held my gaze even as one of her hands clutched mine. Her fingers were cold, almost frigid, while emotion thickened her voice to a hoarse whisper. "You know? You can't know."

"Lori said your husband was less than kind to you."

"It's … it's a complicated situation. Too complicated to explain," she answered.

I glanced around when someone emerged from a cabin and moved in the opposite direction, to where a bathroom was located. "Why don't we go to my cabin? We can talk there."

"No, no, I couldn't. I wouldn't dare," she said, her breath coming fast and hard as her gaze flickered at the carriage door behind me. She reminded me of a gazelle at a watering hole. "Alan is suspicious of everyone. If he knew I was talking to you, if he knew you worked for the Akashic League—no, I just couldn't do that to you. He seldom lets me out of his sight. He thinks I'm sleeping, and if he found me talking to you—if he was aware that you know of my situation, you'd be in terrible danger."

"I appreciate that you feel like you're in a helpless situation, but I assure you that I—"

Movement behind me had me spinning around, my heart in my throat, but it was only Pixie, who had come to see what I was doing.

"Are you OK? I thought you were in the can, but you were taking so long I thought I'd better check to make sure you don't have the trots or something," she said.

"Thank you for your concern, but I'm fine. I was just talking to Rennie—" I turned back while I was speaking, but Rennie was already at the far end of the carriage, her brown-and-beige dress fluttering around her legs as she hurried through the door to the next carriage.

"That was her?" Pixie wrinkled her nose. "She looks like one of those ladies who hang around mortal churches."

Before I could say anything, the door behind Pixie swung open, and Alan Taylor entered, giving both of us a frown until we shifted over so he could pass by in the narrow corridor.

I gripped Pixie's arm as soon as he was past, shooting her a warning look. She squinted at me for a moment before her eyebrows went up, and she leaned out to peer past me at the retreating man.

"That's him?" she asked when he, too, disappeared through the door. "He's got red hair."

"I don't quite see your point," I said, and shooed her back toward the lounge car.

"Whoever heard of a baddie with red hair?"

"If you saw how terrified his wife was, you wouldn't think that."

"What are you going to do?" Pixie asked, pulling out her notebook, obviously poised to take notes.

I thought hard for a few seconds. "About Rennie? Right now, nothing. There's lunch and dinner yet, when we might be able to sit with them. Oh … I don't know if they are at the first or second sitting."

"I'll find out that," she said, scribbling on her notebook. "Paolo is bound to know."

I hesitated a few seconds, then said slowly, "All right, but don't be obvious about it. We don't want him tattling to anyone that we're interested in them."

She tapped her lip with the tip of her pencil, then said, "I'll ask about them and that fancy couple who have the cool outfits."

"What fancy couple?" I asked, looking outside as the train pulled into a small station. We'd been told there would be periodic stops, but that only a few were at the station longer than a minute, and we should stay on board.

"The one a few cars the other way. The woman said her name is Olga, and the dude is Teodor. They were nice, and she had on a black sparkly dress. I'll tell Paolo I want us to sit with them, and that you chatted with Rennie, and liked her. He's our butler, so he has to do what we say, right?"

"He's not a personal body slave, Pixie," I pointed out, but decided she could do no harm. At worst, Paolo might assume she had a mild crush. "I think I'll go back and talk to the Rev some more. He seems to know everyone, and might have insight into Alan Taylor."

"Right. Let's synchronize our watches," Pixie said, pulling out her phone.

"I don't think phones work that way." I tried to hide my amusement, relishing how enthusiastic Pixie was. "But if you like, we can agree to meet in the suite before lunch, OK?"

"All right." She frowned for a moment. "Should I change? Are people going to dress up for lunch the way they will for dinner?"

"I don't think so. You read the information from the train people, so you'd know best. All I remember is that we have to dress nice, and men should wear a suit at dinner."

"I'll change," she said with a note of pleasure in her voice. "I'll make Paolo bring up my big suitcase so I can dig out my *Mummy* librarian costume."

I bit back the rejoinder that she had ample outfits that claimed every available hanger in our shared suite. She'd gone to a lot of trouble to sweet-talk a friend who worked at a local theater company to loan her a few costumes, and I wanted to reward her initiative. "See you later. Mind you don't annoy anyone," I couldn't help but add.

She gave me a haughty curl of her lip. "Deus, Karma! You act like I'm an infant! I don't annoy people. I watch. I record. I detect."

Duly chastised, I returned to the bar compartment, and made my way over to a group of seats where Rev was holding court with an older woman of stout dimensions, and a majestic fake parrot clipped to her bag.

"—and as I said to her, my dear, you are speaking to one who knows, so for you to pretend otherwise is not only an insult to me; it is a slap in the face of spiritualism everywhere." She stopped to give me a piercing look.

"My apologies, I didn't mean to interrupt," I said, feeling a little blush rising under the influence of her steely eyes.

"Not at all," Rev said, patting the love seat next to him, and made quick introductions, adding, "I'm sure Mrs. Summerville won't mind in the least if you join the conversation."

"What about you, gel? Are you psychical?" she demanded, her accent very British upper-class. "Reverend Wall here is a sympathetic, you know. I warn you, I cannot abide skeptics. They suck all the fun out of life. If I had my way, they'd be taken out and left on the moors to die alone and unloved."

I didn't quite know how to respond to that last statement, so I simply said, "I don't think I have any psychic abilities, but I'm very interested in the subject of things beyond the norm."

"Ah. Good." She turned her head slightly and looked over my shoulder. "What about you, young man?"

"What about me?" Alan Taylor had returned. I mentally congratulated myself for guessing that he'd head back to the bar as soon as he was done making sure his wife was cowering in their compartment.

"Do you believe? Or are you one of those naysayers?" Mrs. Summerville said with a derisive sound that I could classify only as a snort. "I was telling Reverend Wall and Miss Mark that I will have nothing to do with anyone who doesn't believe. I am, you see, a true sympathetic. My late husband's family home was riddled with ghosts. Naturally, most of them only appeared to family, but they all showed themselves to me. I remember that my husband was quite taken with that fact at the time."

"Were the spirits at all noisy?" Rev asked, clearly one of those mortals who enjoyed the subject. I'd run into a few of his type before, and normally I steered clear of such conversations—it hit a little too close to home, and I'd found life moved along much more easily if I kept my origins quiet around mortals—but as Alan had gathered another drink and taken possession of the chair on my left, I stayed put. "One of the vicarages I stayed at last summer was haunted by a very evil entity. One could almost say demonic."

"Our family spirits were quite well behaved," Mrs. Summerville said louder than was strictly polite. I wondered if she was a bit hard of hearing. She patted her fake parrot and added, "Geoffrey could always sense when they were near, but they never exuded evilness."

"Did your husband see the spirits, too?" I asked.

"My husband? Of course not. He was a man, and so many men are unbelievers." She gave the two men sitting with us a shared gimlet glance. "Geoffrey was my parrot. He was my familiar, and had a very highly developed sense of *other*."

I couldn't help but cast a look of horror at the parrot, realizing that what I'd assumed was a somewhat eccentric accessory was actually a stuffed bird.

"Men have just as much an ability to see spirits as women." We all turned to look at Alan as he stopped a passing attendant and asked for another drink. When he noticed our collective attention, he gave a little shrug. "Well, they can. I've known several men who had interactions with ghosts. What I don't get is why so many people think they're evil. No offense, Reverend Wall, but your demonic entity was probably just some lonely spirit who was misunderstood."

"With all due respect, you weren't there," Rev said gently. "As a man of faith, I am familiar with the brush of evil. I see it in far too many places. It is the age-old battle of the benign against that which is malignant through and through."

"That's a very black-and-white sort of thinking," Alan argued, making a face. "And by saying that, I intend no reference to racial differences."

Rev murmured that he understood and took no offense.

"So many people think that what's depicted on their TVs and in movies is real that they don't understand that spirits are just like living people—there are shades of gray," Alan continued. "Sure, there are bad spirits who want to harm the living, but there are also people who have a mixture of good and bad in them. Sometimes one facet wins out, and becomes dominant."

"I have seen more evil in the hearts of man than I ever have in the spirit world," Mrs. Summerville announced, jerking Geoffrey the parrot upright when it sagged against Rev's leg. "And I have never seen proof of a spirit wishing to kill someone, which I believe is usually the standard fare out of Hollywood."

Pixie entered the carriage and caught my eye, pulling one edge of a notebook from her bag, indicating, I assumed, that she had the info we needed. I gave her a quick nod when she made a couple of vague gestures that no doubt meant she wanted to join the conversation but wasn't sure if I'd welcome her.

"I'm pleased to say that I have not met with any murderous ghosties, either," the Rev said somewhat playfully, "although there were some very naughty poltergeists at a house in the north of Scotland. I was visiting an old friend, and one evening we were sitting quietly by the fire, and suddenly, out of the blue, a book flew off the shelf and landed at my friend's feet. I was quite surprised, as you can imagine, but he told me that sort of thing happened all the time, and that it was the poltergeists that inhabited the house who delighted in playing such tricks on him."

"That's not a polter," Pixie said as she stopped in front of me. "Polters don't do that."

"Ah, you say that, but had you been in such a situation, I'm confident that you, too, would have been aware of the otherness of that evening," Rev said with a friendly smile.

Pixie sniffed. "I don't need to be there to know it's not polters who go around flinging books all over the place. I mean, that's just stupid. Why would they do that?"

A silence fell over our little group for a second before I stood up and put an arm around her. "This is my foster daughter, Pixie," I introduced her, then, turning her toward the direction she'd just come, said, "Goodness, is that the time? We have a few things to do before lunch."

"What an odd young gel," Mrs. Summerville said, holding Geoffrey up in a manner that indicated she was allowing him to view Pixie, as well. "Is she wearing jodhpurs?"

"I like to see the young indulging in their right to question those of us who have a few more years under our belts," Rev said placidly. "No doubt she will learn with time to open her mind to those experiences that we have witnessed with our own eyes."

"Karma! I'm not a baby," Pixie whispered harshly when I hustled her down the aisle, past the now almost-full lounge car. People wore everything from standard tourist wear—albeit of a higher standard than the normal T-shirts and shorts of others I'd seen in Paris—to a few period pieces. Clearly we were not alone in having a wardrobe that catered to the atmosphere of the train.

"Sorry, I just wanted to get us out of that situation before one of us said something that we'd regret." I released the grip I had on Pixie's arm, and allowed her to precede me down the length of three sleeping carriages until we got to the one bearing our suite.

"Why did you do that?" she demanded to know once I closed the door behind us. "That old man was talking bullshit about us."

"He was talking about the Hollywood idea of poltergeists, not actual polters, and I stopped you because the confident manner in which you disputed the Reverend Wall had caught Alan Taylor's attention. And that's the last thing we need. What did you find out from Paolo?"

She had been working herself up to being offended over being removed from what I considered a dangerous situation, but immediately donned a canny expression. "Alan Taylor is at the second seating."

"Crap. We'll have to switch."

"I had Paolo change us to that one. Did you find out anything from Hitty McHitterson?" She plopped down onto the sofa, stretching out on it, making a face when I made her move her boots off the lovely upholstery.

"If you are referring to Alan Taylor, not much other than he has a surprising take on spirits, considering his wife is a vespillo."

"So, about these necromancers." She stopped texting a friend to ask, "Do they summon skeletons?"

"No, they are exactly what I told you before: they use the essence that vespillos find and then summon the spirit into a corporeal form."

"Yeah, but you never said how they look. Do they have, like, rotting flesh dripping off them? Are their guts spilling out of their partially decayed bones? Can you see their brains pulse with life?"

I pointed a finger at her. "Don't make me put a child lock on your Netflix profile. No to all of those. The spirits look no different than a mortal."

"Oh." She lost interest and returned to tapping on her phone. "So what do we do now?"

"Now we find out which of the three dining cars lunch will be held in, and lurk around to see where Alan and Rennie sit. With luck, it will be at a table for four, and we can join them. If they sit in one of the two-seaters, we'll have to park ourselves opposite and eavesdrop like crazy."

"Why do you want to have lunch with them so badly?" she asked, watching me over the top of her phone when I cracked open one of the bottles of sparkling water that Paolo had left in our drinks rack, and poured out a glass. She shook her head when I picked up a second glass.

"For two reasons. One, I feel like establishing a relationship could cast us in a less sinister light. Rennie said Alan was suspicious of everyone, but if we are constantly bumping into them and chatting with them, then he won't think anything of it if he sees me having a casual conversation with her."

"I suppose that makes sense. What's the second reason?"

I sipped at the water, watching the scenery blur past us, the bubbles feeling oddly unpleasant in my stomach.

"I want him to know we're aware of Rennie."

Pixie was silent a moment before she asked, "Do you think he might try to hurt her? Here on the train?"

"I don't know. I fervently hope not. But if he does, I want him to know that others have talked to her and will notice if anything happens."

"You have depths," Pixie told me, then got to her feet and picked up one of her garment bags before taking it into the en suite bathroom. She paused at the door, looking over her shoulder at me. "Seriously dark depths. You might want to get some therapy for that."

"True words," I said softly to the door that she had closed, then sat down with a small notebook of my own, and made notes.

FIVE

"You must be Karma."

I looked up at the man who stood at the open compartment door, looking in. Pixie and I had heard at lunch from a middle-aged pair of twin sisters who sat at our table—Alan Taylor not bothering to attend the restaurant car—that it was standard to leave your door open if you wished to indicate a willingness to chat with other travelers. Since I thought that was a perfect excuse to keep an eye out for both Rennie and Alan, I had settled down with a book in our suite, and chatted with those who passed by.

"I am," I said, sliding a bookmark into a compendium of a copy of Christie's *Murder of Roger Ackroyd*, one of my favorite books.

"I am Teodor Palaiologos," the man said, making a formal bow. He was dressed in a lovely navy-and-cream vintage suit and wore his hair in a style that was reminiscent of the early 1920s. "And this is the Princess Olga Mikhailovna."

"Good afternoon," a woman said as Teodor moved slightly the side. Like him, she was dressed in period wear, a gorgeous flaming-red flapper dress decorated with elaborate gold beading, and matching scarlet marabou feathers. Her blonde hair wasn't bobbed, but undulated in waves from her brow back to a tidy bun at the nape of her neck. "You may call me Olga. I do not use the title so much anymore. Your daughter … no, that is not the right word. Teo?"

"Ward?" he suggested.

"Your ward, Pixie, told us about you. You permit?"

"Of course," I said, feeling all shades of rude. I'd risen when Olga entered, and hurriedly waved them toward the long sofa. "How delightful to meet you both. I don't believe I've had the pleasure of meeting an actual princess before. Er … of what country … ?"

"Russia," Olga said. "The original one, not the one with all the Communists."

I didn't quite know what to say to that, so, mindful of Paolo's promise that we were afforded free-flowing (and gratis by account of the expensive suite) champagne, I pressed one of the bells that summoned him. "You'll have some champagne, I hope?"

"That would be quite pleasant," Olga said, beaming at me. "Teodor is Hungarian."

"Also from before the Communists," he said with a husky laugh.

Paolo appeared in the door. "Champagne, please, Paolo."

"Ah, for you and the signorina? It will be just one moment."

"Three glasses, please," I told him, wondering why he would assume Pixie and I would guzzle champers in front of our two guests.

We chatted for a few minutes about the part of Switzerland we were traveling through, and I asked if they were here for the mystery event.

"We love it," Teodor said, his Eastern European accent almost lyrical. "We make sure that we never miss it."

Obviously, they must be well-off if they could afford the trip each year. I said nothing when Paolo entered with the champagne, popped the cork, then poured a little out for me to taste. When I had done so, he filled my flute, but left the other two empty.

I stared at him as he left the compartment, about to offer an excuse for his apparent rudeness, but that's when the penny dropped.

Teodor and Olga sat smiling gently, pleasant anticipation evident on their faces.

"You're … you're …" I stopped when a couple passed by the corridor, calling out a greeting. I answered quickly before turning back to look at my guests. "You're spirits."

"Of course we are," Olga said, eyeing the champagne.

"Corporeal spirits." I studied them for a few seconds. "You're not bound to this train."

"That we are not," Teodor said.

I realized they were waiting very patiently, and poured out two glasses of champagne, which they both accepted with murmured thanks.

"Very good vintage," Teodor said, toasting his companion.

"Quite drinkable, although a shade too dry for my taste," Olga replied.

I stared at the open door for a minute, my thoughts whirling around until two of them slotted together. "I take it that since you aren't grounded to the train, but are corporeal, that you did not die here?"

"Actually, we did, but luckily, a very nice Summoner released us so that we could visit old haunts," Teodor said, smiling broadly when I topped up his glass. "Mind you, Budapest has changed, and I'm not sure for the better, but still, it's nice for us to get out now and again. Olga particularly loves Istanbul."

"It brings back so many happy memories," she said with a smile that hinted of long-past pleasures. "My late husband and I spent many happy times there before the revolution. But such happy memories are not why we are here. We have something of much import to tell you. We told Pixie, but I do not have confidence that she took the information seriously."

"Oh?" I sat down, still holding the champagne bottle, smiling and nodding when a group of three women paused at the door.

"Karma! June and Allison and I are going to the lounge for the murder-mystery briefing. Did you want to join us? We're going to get the scoop on what to look for and how to find the killer so that those Brits don't beat us to the punch."

"Thanks, but Pixie and I were planning on attending the later session," I told the ladies.

"Yeah, because they're going to have a real homicide detective there from Vienna," Pixie said, popping up in front of the group before scooting past them to our suite. "I have, like, a billion questions for him. Oh hi."

"We should work together," Donna, the tourist, said in a conspiratorial tone as her two companions continued on. "My sisters aren't the brightest pennies in the gumball machine, if you get my drift. You and Pixie are clearly committing yourselves to the whole thing with your great costumes. It was all I could do to get June to part with one of her beloved pantsuits in order to wear a slightly vintage-looking dress, and don't get me started about Allison's idea of what's appropriate for evening wear. She has four ex-husbands, you know."

"I didn't know, but I'm sure their costumes are just fine," I said a bit desperately, pulling the door toward me in hopes that I could close it before she told me more of her life story. "And I have no doubt that several people will be working together to solve the mystery."

"Not committing yourself beforehand, eh? Can't say that I blame you, but don't judge me by my sisters. I'm a whole lot more sophisticated than them. My husband got out well before the tech bubble burst, and theirs didn't." She tapped the side of her nose and winked, which had me believing she'd been at the free-flowing champagne a little early, then hurried after the others, calling out, "June, if you hog that nice Mr. Taylor again, I swear I'll hide your denture cream!"

I had the door closed before Donna had finished speaking.

"I like her," Pixie said, plopping down in one of the two deep armchairs. "She says what she thinks, and doesn't care who hears her. She told that snobby English lady that her dead bird smelled funky. Can we have dinner here? My glamour is itching, and I want to drop it for a bit."

"Dinner isn't for another two hours, but go ahead and take off the glamour," I told her before switching my attention to our visitors, who had snagged the bottle and were just finishing it. "What exactly is it you wanted to tell me?"

"Oh, that." Pixie gave one of her trademark eye rolls and unzipped the garment bag that hung on the door of the bathroom. "Honestly, Karma, it's nothing. Like, less than nothing. Just a ghost. Do you think I'll look older if I wear my tuxedo suit for the Austrian detective? Or should I go for the lounging pajamas?"

"Oooh, what color are they?" Olga asked, leaning forward to see around Teodor.

"Peacock," Pixie said, then took the bag itself in when she disappeared into the bathroom.

"Peacock," Olga repeated, running a hand around the marabou on her neckline. "I have not tried that color, I think. Teo?"

"Not since I've known you," he said, leaning to the side in order to consider her. "I don't know that the color would suit you. You're very blond, and Pixie is not. Perhaps a soft sky blue, instead."

"I do like that shade," she told him. "My mother—she was Queen Victoria's granddaughter, you know—she always favored that color, and told me I could never go wrong with it. But of course, I was a young girl, and young girls do not listen to their parents."

"That is so frequently true," Teodor agreed, and both turned to look at me. "What do you think, Karma?"

"About sky blue, peacock blue, or teens ignoring the wisdom of their elders?" I gave a little shake of my head. "Honestly, I don't particularly care about any of that. What I do want to know is what has Pixie trying to convince me is nothing. What ghost is she talking about?"

"Hervé," Teodor said, then looked wistfully at the empty bottle.

"No more. I don't want Paolo thinking I killed a bottle in ten minutes," I told them.

They both sighed, but made themselves comfortable on the sofa nonetheless.

"Hervé is in car H, compartment five," Olga said, smoothing out the chiffon skirt of her dress. "He also died on the train."

"Was there an accident?" I asked, confused as to why there would be three ghosts on a single train.

"You could say that," she answered, then waved a hand at Teodor. "Teo's brother Johan was having a party that night."

"He'd just gotten engaged to a minor German royal. She was not, how shall I say, overly enticing, you know? Her father was exiled, of course, but somehow had convinced the government to pay him for his land before the socialists came into power, and she lusted after Johan, so he agreed to marry her."

"Not before she was in a difficult situation," Olga murmured, her gaze on her hands.

"The party was very exciting, you understand," Teodor continued. "There was much champagne, many ladies and gentlemen, and even a four-piece band. We had dancing, and drinking, and much gambling."

"I'm a bit surprised the train people allowed that," I said.

Teodor shrugged. "They did not care until the lover joined the train in Zurich."

"What lover?" I asked, intrigued despite knowing I should remain focused.

"The woman's lover. It was he who fathered her indisposition," Olga said, her eyes a bright blue, almost unnaturally blue. It reminded me how much I preferred the pale blue of Adam's eyes. "The father said that he could not marry her because he was a government official, and the woman's father was still silky about being exiled."

"Silky?" I asked.

"Salty, dear one," Teodor told her, then when he saw my surprise at his use of slang, added, "We hear much on the train, and try to stay current with what is happening."

"Gotcha. So the fiancée's boyfriend showed up. I take it he had a few things to say to your brother."

"Many things," Teodor said with a little smile. "And then he challenged Johan to a duel."

"On the train?" I couldn't help but stop at the idea of anyone doing something so stupid in the closed confines of a railroad car.

"Of course." He shrugged. "Unfortunately, Johan shot the lover's arm, and he went mad, and in the end, Olga, two train attendants, Hervé, and I were dead."

"Holy shitsnacks," I said, using one of Pixie's favorite oaths. "How horrible for you."

"It is not as bad as you might think," Olga said, using the toe of her shoe to nudge the stand holding the empty champagne bottle, which I ignored. I had no desire to make the staff of the Byzantine Express believe I was a drunkard on my first day on the train. "My husband was dead by that time—shot in the revolution, you know—and my then-lover was starting to look elsewhere for affection, so I had no ties there. Teo and I enjoy ourselves here, and as I said, we can visit any of the cities en route."

"But we don't often get champagne, except those times when the company hosts fancy dress parties," Teodor added.

"Ah, I think I see. You mingle then, yes? But … if you can go corporeal, surely you can change your outfits."

"And so we do," Olga said, brushing her hand down her dress again before fluffing up a bit of marabou. "I will be wearing a stunning black velvet gown tomorrow night at the murder party."

"And I will have on my Order of St. George," Teodor said.

"I look forward to seeing both, but you haven't explained the problem with the other ghost—wait, what happened to the two attendants who also died?"

"The Summoner said they preferred to go dormant," Teodor said. "Hervé was different. He wanted to be grounded immediately."

"So you and this Hervé are grounded, can be corporeal when you desire, but not bound to the train?"

"We aren't bound, but Hervé decided that he would stay put." Olga exchanged a look with Teodor just as Pixie emerged from the bathroom wearing a pair of silk blue lounging pajamas embroidered with intricate scroll details.

"He is unhappy," Teodor said while Olga rose to go admire Pixie's outfit. The latter did a twirl for her, telling her she'd found it in a local antique clothing shop.

"Unhappy about being on the train, or being killed?" I asked, one eye on Pixie as Olga examined the embroidered sleeve.

"Unhappy with everything. Especially women," he said, crossing his legs and leaning back, a thoughtful expression clouding his brown eyes a little. "He dislikes women greatly, you understand. He blames his death on my brother's bride, since it was because of her that her lover lost his hinge."

It took me a minute to grasp his word usage. "So because the lover became unhinged and killed Hervé and you guys, he's angry with women? Does he frighten them?"

"If only it was that," Olga said, returning to her seat. "But he is not happy until he can, as he says, remove the threat that women pose to all men who just wish to travel on the train in peace and quiet. He is very adamant about the peace and quiet."

"I went to car H," Pixie said, picking up her phone before plunking down on the chair again. "I didn't see anything, let alone a pissy ghost."

"It is not safe, *ma petite*," Olga said, her voice dropping to a whisper. "Hervé, he hates women. He wants to see all of us gone from the train. Me, he tolerates because I was killed, too, but all others are not safe."

"Does he yell at women passengers, then?" I asked, still unclear as to what the problem was with the ghost other than a general bad attitude.

"No, he attacks." Teodor made a stabbing gesture, as if he were running someone through with a sword. "He spends most of his time in the shadows."

"Incorporeal," Olga said, pronouncing the word carefully.

"Yes, that. He spends his time watching and waiting, and if a woman is assigned his compartment, then he will strike blows upon her."

"He opens the window, and throws the woman's things out of it," Olga added.

"Twice, he tried to strangle women passengers. Luckily, both times, the husbands, they woke up in time, and he was forced to retreat again to the shadows."

"Incorporeal," Olga whispered.

My blood ran cold at the description of the maniac ghost. "He sounds like he's out of control. Has no one from the Akashic League ever tried to stop him?"

"No," Teodor said simply. "He hides if anyone like you—or Pixie—shows unless you go into his compartment. And then poof! He will attack. That is why we warn you."

"Is there a woman in there now? A mortal woman, I mean?" I asked, wondering if I shouldn't talk to Paolo about the situation.

"No, no, the company, they made a rule some years ago that no woman was to stay in that compartment. It is for the mens only," Olga said. "We heard the attendants talking about it … what was it, Teo, ten years ago?"

"Twelve, I think," he said, nodding, his golden curls bobbing gently with the movement. "Not even the female attendants are allowed in there, because Hervé struck one on the head, and there was blood everywhere."

"He wasn't there when I peeked into the compartment," Pixie said, pulling out an earbud.

I cocked an eyebrow at her in a manner that had her bristling. "I trust that I don't have to forbid you to go into that compartment again."

"I'm not a mortal woman, Karma," Pixie said with blithe disregard.

"No, but you can be hurt, and I don't need to add worry about you getting into a fight with a misogynistic ghost on top of everything else we're dealing with."

"Dealing with?" Teodor asked at the same time that Olga demanded to know, "What are you dealing with? Something to do with the train? A passenger?"

"Yes, but it's not anything that we're at liberty to talk about," I told them with a warning look at Pixie. She had both earbuds in again, and was obviously texting with a friend back home. "Later, perhaps, but right now I can't. I do want to thank you, however, for warning us about Hervé."

They rose in the face of my not-so-gracious indication that our conversation time was over.

"But of course. We would warn anyone who was in danger, although most of the passengers tend to not listen to us."

"The old madame with the bird, she listens," Teodor said. "She is a bit, what do you say, Lady Gaga in the head?"

"I don't know if she's Lady Gaga, but she is certainly eccentric," I answered, a bit surprised that they had trotted around in corporeal form, but decided that was none of my business.

They took their leave after another minute's chat about the mystery event the following night, and I closed the compartment door after them with a sense of exhaustion that had nothing to do with residual jet lag, and everything to do with too many concerns.

"And why the hell hasn't Adam answered any of my texts?" I fretted, pulling out my own phone to see if I had missed a notification.

"You said he was at a trial. They probably took his phone and stuff," Pixie pointed out, reclaiming the couch. "Going to take a nap."

"Fine, but keep your cape handy in case Paolo comes in to tidy," I said, and went into the bathroom to freshen up a bit.

When I returned, Pixie was curled up with her voluminous black velvet cape serving as a blanket. "What are you going to do?" she asked.

"Hang around various cars and try to find Rennie. Don't forget we're spending the night at the hotel in Vienna, so pack your overnight bag appropriately."

"I don't see why we have this nice compartment if we have to spend every other night at a hotel," she complained, snuggling down into the velvet cloak.

"It's part of the mystique of the train or something," I said, then headed out to the lounge car, hoping that my luck would change and I'd run into Rennie on her own.

SIX

Luck, I've found, is seldom on my side, and this time was no different.

It wasn't until the following day, when everyone had rejoined the train fresh from a night at an expensive hotel, that I saw Rennie again.

The lounge car was busier than normal, since a new batch of tourists joined the journey in progress. I gathered they wanted a less expensive trip, while still being able to participate in the murder-mystery party, but since my attention was focused elsewhere, I didn't give the newcomers much other than polite greetings.

As the first-sitting people began to filter into the lounge car, I headed toward the car where we were lunching that day, hoping to see Rennie.

"How was your stay at the Hotel Sauberwald?" Rev asked, appearing next to me as I paused at the restaurant-car entrance.

At the far end of the car, I could see Alan Taylor's red hair. He was seated at one of the tables for two, and as I watched, Rennie emerged from the door behind him and stood, glancing hesitantly toward her husband. She was clad in the same dress she'd worn the day before, and had a general air of distress that was evident even to me.

"Karma?" Rev asked, a gentle cough behind me warning me that others were piling up behind us.

"Sorry, I was just trying to remember if I left something behind at the hotel. It was lovely, wasn't it? Pixie particularly enjoyed the huge tub. I had to bribe her with Sacher torte in order to get her out. If you'll excuse me, I see someone I'd like to have a quick word with …"

I hurried off down the aisle before he could say anything, intending on corralling Rennie for a chat.

Just as I approached Alan, Rennie gave a sobbing gasp and, with her head down, turned and fled out of the car toward the nonsuite sleeping cars.

I paused for a few seconds, wondering if I should go after her, or tackle Alan. I decided that I'd give Rennie a few moments to collect herself.

Alan scowled as I slipped into the seat opposite him, determined to figure out a few things. "Oh, it's you," he said, a sour look on his face.

"Yes. I hope you don't mind if I sit here, since your wife apparently isn't joining you."

"My wife?" His scowl deepened as he pinned me back with a look that I would have been worried about had I not heard how he treated Rennie. "Why are you talking about my wife?"

"I'm concerned about Rennie. About her well-being." I decided that a little laying of cards on the table might be productive, if in no other way than making it perfectly clear that people were not blind to his treatment of her.

"Concerned?" he repeated, his face flaming red with obvious anger. Words shot out with the velocity of bullets, aimed directly at me. "Are you insane? Just who the hell are you, and how do you know Rennie?"

"You know my name," I countered, feeling a bit panicky about how furious he was. His voice hadn't risen at all despite his emotion, but I still felt like I'd been pinned to the back of the chair by the animosity rolling off him. "As it happens, I don't know her well. But I'm a member of the Akashic League, and—"

"Christ," he said on a near snarl, one hand combing his hair back with agitated, jerky movements. "You're one of them."

"I'm not a necromancer, if that's what you mean. Or even a vespillo. I'm an exterminator."

He leaned forward over the table, his voice so low I could barely hear it, but it fairly dripped with warning. "I don't know what you're trying to do, but stay away from Rennie. Do you hear me? Stay away from her. From me. I won't be responsible for any harm that comes to you if you mess with her."

"You are seriously over the line," I said, shocked at the threat.

"No, you are," he said, his voice a growl that had goose bumps rippling down my arms. "What's worse, you're an idiot if you think that you will come out of this unscathed. Just leave Rennie alone."

"I will not tolerate abuse—"

"Do you have a death wish, or are you really that stupid?" he said, but rose and stormed out of the carriage before I could answer.

"Merciful heaven," came a soft murmur from behind me. I turned back from where I was looking over my shoulder, unsure if I should chase down Alan Taylor and demand to know why he was so upset about me talking with Rennie. Rev stood before me, his hands clasped over his stomach, a question in his gaze. "That was most unlike Mr. Taylor."

"Wasn't it," I said softly, accepting a menu card that a waiter offered.

"Is the delightful Pixie joining you?" Rev asked, nodding toward Alan's now-empty chair.

"No, she's taking some me time in our room. You're welcome to join me if you like," I said politely, although I very much wished to spend time thinking about what to do next. Talking with Rennie privately was at the top of the list.

"I'd be delighted to join you if you're sure I'm not intruding," Rev said, seating himself, and picking up the menu card that Alan Taylor had dropped when he saw me. "Ah, *le blanc de St. Pierre poêlé et la cristalline de coppa. Frottée au sel de Guérande. Le jus aux essences de carottes et d'oranges.* One of my favorites. Is that what you'd like, as well?"

I glanced at the card and read the translation (white and green asparagus creamy soup with buffalo mozzarella toast; sautéed chicken oysters and diced tomatoes with basil), and shook my head. "I think I'll have the chicken breast with morel sauce. I feel spoiled by the choices, though. There's so many dishes here that I'd love to try."

"The *chef de cuisine* is talented," Rev agreed. We gave our orders, and spent ten minutes chatting about the trip thus far before our meals arrived.

"This is, quite obviously, none of my business, but if there's anything you wish to confide in me, I assure you that I take seriously the sanctity of confession." Rev glanced around and, with a little wink at me, dipped a bit of bread into his asparagus soup before popping the piece into his mouth.

"Oh. I … uh … I didn't know you were Catholic," I said, mildly confused.

His eyes widened. "I'm not. Oh, confession? The Church of England tends to practice general confession during normal services, but it's not unknown to seek a one-on-one with a priest. However, what I was referring to was more a sharing of mental burdens rather than an actual confession to transgressions you may have committed." He beamed at me, his eyes filled with amused warmth. "Although I'm sure a woman as caring as you couldn't possibly have any actual sin to confess. I thought you might wish to talk about Mr. Taylor's accusations, which unfortunately I overheard as I approached."

I poked at my chicken (which was insanely delicious, and made a mental note to find out what Pixie had ordered for her lunch in our suite) and thought to myself that the Rev had no idea with what sins my soul was burdened. "That's thoughtful of you, but I assure you that I don't need a shoulder to cry on. Mr. Taylor was upset by an inquiry I made about his wife, that's all."

"Ah," he said, chewing thoughtfully. "You are a friend of Mrs. Taylor?"

"We have a mutual acquaintance," I said with what I hoped was nonchalance, and tried my best to change the conversation. "Are you looking forward to the event tonight?"

"Very much so, as well as our stop this afternoon at Lake Balaton, although I believe I will forgo the boat ride on the lake."

"You're not a good sailor?" I asked, smiling.

He shook his head, and clutched at his stomach, grimacing for a few seconds. "Very much not, dear lady.

I shall instead take a stroll around the lake, and then return to my compartment and prepare for the evening's event. What of you and your ward?"

I hesitated, unsure that I wanted to commit myself to any action. "Pixie's whims are frequently prone to change at the last minute, so I'll have to wait and see what she feels like."

"Indeed, I've found that the young often change their plans at the drop of a hat. Not like those of us who are older and wiser, eh? Take Mr. Taylor, now. He is a man who is obviously set in his ways, and doesn't take well to people breaching his boundaries."

I eyed Rev, wondering if he, too, was giving me a warning. And if so, why?

"He strikes me as an intensely private man," Rev continued, his gaze filled with mild inquiry. "Not at all the sort of person who is agreeable on this sort of a trip, where one is forced to rely upon the forthcoming nature of one's fellow travelers to pass the time, eh?"

"Some people don't like to perform for others," I said carefully.

His eyebrows rose. "That is so, that is so," he agreed, leaning back so the waiter could whisk away his plate and replace it with an empty one in preparation for cheese or a sweet confection. "But it seemed to me that his comments toward you were more of a threatening nature than a polite refusal to discuss something personal."

"You really did overhear quite a bit of the conversation," I said, holding his gaze for a few seconds before he dropped his, picking up a spoon to tackle the orange custard placed there. I wondered if he'd heard the part before Alan Taylor started spouting off at me, and mentally chastised myself for being so focused on him that I hadn't noticed anyone standing in the aisle close enough to us to hear.

"Enough that I find myself worried about you. If you take the boat trip on Lake Balaton, I urge you to use caution should Mr. Taylor be present, as well. It is also why I am happy to offer myself as a guide should you wish to take a stroll around the lake instead."

"That's very kind of you. No, nothing, thank you. Please pass along my compliments to the chef. The chicken was the best I've ever had." The last few sentences were spoken to the waiter, who looked pleased and promised to pass along my praise as he cleared away my dishes, and deposited a small cup of very strong coffee.

"It is the least I can do," Rev said, his face crinkling a little as he smiled and touched his collar. "Man of the cloth, and all that."

"Thank you," I said, rising. "I appreciate the offer and warning, and if Pixie and I decide to pass on the boat trip, I'll take you up on the offer of protection. But now I really should go check and make sure she's not using up all the hot water."

He laughed as I hurried off, my mind whirling with threats, hints, and all sorts of confusion about … well, just about everything.

"The question is, why is the Rev warning us?" I asked ten minutes later as I paced up and down our compartment. "He seemed awfully chatty with Alan Taylor yesterday, and now he's warning us about him? It doesn't make sense. Not unless he has an ulterior motive."

"You've got ulterior motives on the brain," Pixie said, lying on her back on the sofa. Her boots were off, I was pleased to note, but she held a book above her face, clearly annoyed that I had interrupted her. "Can you, like, take a nap or go grill someone? Because I want to finish this book before tonight, so I can figure out who the murderer is before everyone else."

"Do I take it you don't want to go on the lake cruise?" I asked, still pacing.

"Ugh. With a bunch of old people? I'd rather have to walk around without a glamour."

"Those very same people are on this train, you know."

"I know, but at least here, they are all potential suspects," she answered, turning a page.

"Fine. I'll go haunt the corridors hoping to find Rennie without her violent husband," I said, a bit exasperated.

She lowered the book enough to peer over it at me. "Are you going to go see that anti-woman ghost?"

"Of course not. The last thing I need is to upset a spirit."

"You could bump him off the train," she pointed out. "Teodor said that they wouldn't tell anyone if you did that. Olga says Hervé has it coming."

"I am not exterminating anyone. For one, it's not my place to do so. And for another—" I held up my wrist to show my monitor. "If you recall, I'm forbidden to do anything but take care of a few vermin. And don't give me that innocent look. You are not to go into that cabin, Pixie. I don't even want you in car H."

"Deus, do you get off on bossing me around? I heard you the first time! Now let me read or I won't see how Hercule Poirot figures out who killed the baddie." She returned to her book, using one hand to shoo me.

I left with one last warning to steer clear of the carriage, and emerged to see Rennie standing at the end of my corridor, where a chair sat for the night attendant.

She rocked with the train as we wound our way out of Austria and into Hungary, holding on to the window as she gazed out at the passing green fields.

I hurried up, glancing around, but there was no one at either end of the car, and the doors to the three suites were all closed. "Rennie! I'm so glad to see you. How are you?"

"I'm well, thank you," she said politely, but her gaze dropped to her hands.

"I saw you earlier, at lunch."

"Yes. Alan … my husband said you were there. Said that you had spoken about me." She looked up, her eyes filled with tears, her hand cold on mine as she grabbed it. "Oh, Karma, you don't know what you've done. Alan is … he has always hated the Otherworld. And now he knows you're a part of it."

I said nothing for a moment, wondering if she knew he had been at G&T a few nights past. Was he keeping secrets from her? Or was she trying to make me believe something that wasn't true? But if it was the latter, why? What purpose would it serve to make me think he hated the Otherworld?

I gave a mental headshake. It didn't make sense. But it wouldn't hurt to probe a little. "Why does he have such strong feelings about it?" I asked. "Is he weirded out by it?"

"No, he's … oh, it's just that he's so controlling, you know? He doesn't like anything he can't dominate or command, and everything in the Otherworld is beyond that."

"I suppose some people could feel that way about those of us in the Otherworld. But to be honest, I'm more concerned about you and your safety than your husband's feelings," I said bluntly. "I want to help you,

Rennie. And I think if we can get you away from your husband—"

"Oh, I couldn't do that." Her eyes were huge before she turned and looked out the window again, her fingers now white as she clutched the window frame. "I appreciate your desire to help, but it's far too dangerous. You don't know how bad Alan can be. I've been so worried that no one would believe me that I started recording him on my phone without his knowledge."

"I'm not sure that's legal, although I understand you wanting to have proof," I said slowly, mindful of what Adam would say in that situation.

It made me miss him that much more, and I spent a second pushing down the sadness that he wasn't there with me, helping to untangle the mess that faced us.

"Proof, yes, that's what I wanted. Proof just in case he did something to harm someone innocent."

"If you have a recording, then you can take it to the Watch. Or the Akashic League, since you're a member," I told her. "Even if the recording wouldn't be able to be used to convict him, it does offer evidence you are in danger."

"But I don't have the phone anymore," she said on a near wail, turning toward me, wringing her hands. "Alan found it and took it from me. He has it somewhere in his luggage, hidden where I can't find it."

"It's here? On the train?" I asked, hope filling me at a plan that was audacious, if highly illegal.

"Yes, but as I said, it's hidden. Alan is very devious when it comes to that. I've tried looking for it, but he lays little traps with his belongings to see if anything has been moved."

"Do you give me permission to enter your compartment and search your belongings?" I said, making a decision. I knew full well that the League would take a dim view of me getting involved in work that by rights was in the Watch's line, but I wasn't about to let that bother me. Not if it meant helping Rennie escape her abuser. "Do you allow me to look at the videos on your phone?"

"Yes, of course, but that won't help you with Alan's things. His are—"

I held up a hand to stop her. "Don't tell me which are his and which are yours. That way I can honestly say that I didn't know."

"Oh." She thought about that for a moment, then said, "I suppose that makes sense, but really, Karma, it's far too dangerous. I can't allow you to put yourself in such a perilous situation. If Alan found you there—if he knew you were working to help me—I couldn't live with myself if he harmed you."

"Don't worry about that. I'm not as feeble as I look," I told her.

She looked over my shoulder, her face pale as she leaned closer and said softly, "You mustn't let him catch you. He's violent. He has a horrible temper, and he never forgives those who he thinks have wronged him."

"I'm well aware of his temper," I said, glancing behind me. Rev and Mrs. Summerville were working their way down the corridor. "But I'll—" I turned back, but Rennie was gone, the blue velvet cloth that swathed the train car connectors moving slightly with her passing.

I hurried after her, not wanting to get engaged in conversation again, and spent some time snooping around the various public cars looking for Alan Taylor or Rennie, but neither was in evidence. By the time we stopped at Lake Balaton, I had a plan that I fervently hoped wouldn't backfire.

"You're sure you don't want to go to the lake?" I asked Pixie as I gathered up a book, my bag, and a sun hat.

"Do I look like I'm eighty?" she asked, now sitting at the table, her book propped up on a bottle of fizzy water. She looked up to add, "Paolo says they have absinthe at the bar. Can I get a glass at the party tonight?"

"Would your lady archaeologist drink something so bohemian?" I asked, lining up a whole plethora of excuses to keep her away from hard liquor.

She wrinkled her nose and looked thoughtful for a few seconds. "She might."

"She strikes me as more a ginger beer sort of character," I said, mentally crossing my fingers.

"Ginger beer? What's that?" she asked, looking faintly suspicious. "Is it ginger ale?"

"No, it's alcoholic, although they have a nonalcoholic version. I had some of the former with lunch. It was good, although it gave me a bit of a buzz."

That last was a blatant lie, but I hoped it would channel Pixie's desires from a beverage I considered beyond her years even if Europe as a whole felt it was fine.

"Hmm. She might be that sort of person. She's not a snob," Pixie said, musing. "Unlike her rich benefactors who pay for her archaeological digs, she's a woman of the people. She spurns the trappings of wealth. What are you doing? Are you following Alan Taylor? Are you going to hide in the shadows and track him like the beast he is?"

"None of those." I told her briefly about my conversation with Rennie.

"Deus!" she said, her eyes big. "You're going to steal the phone?"

"*Steal* is an extreme word—"

"Can I do it, too?" She set down her book, waving her arms with excitement. "I can help you search their stuff. Or maybe—oooh, I have a better idea. Why don't we wait until tonight when they're asleep, and we can slip into their compartment and go polter on him! We can both flicker at him, and I'll do that creepy Japanese-horror-movie thing with my hair over my face. We'll scare the crap out of him and when he runs away screaming, we'll find Rennie's phone."

"No," I said. "And don't you even think about getting indignant about me not allowing you to do something that is highly questionable at best, and illegal as hell at worst."

"It may be illegal, but you're doing it for a righteous cause," she said, looking stubborn. "That counts."

"It does, but only insofar as I'm willing to risk the repercussions of being found in the Taylors' compartment. I am not willing to put you at risk for the same thing."

"You're no fun," she said, sniffing to herself as she reclaimed her book. "You want my life to be boring and stupid. I only have two more years with you, you know. Then I'm out from under the dictatorship of you and the Home."

"You can revolt at that time," I said placidly. "Until then, keep your nose clean."

"Ew. Gross."

I stuffed a few things into my bag and said, "Are you going to have dinner here or in the restaurant car?"

I thought she was giving me the silent treatment for a minute, but finally, she unbent. "Here. Paolo said that Carlo, the chef, would make me his special Charolais beef with tarragon and sun-dried tomato. He doesn't make that for everyone, but he said that since I'd given him five stars on the sea bass with braised-fennel fondue that I had for lunch, he'd make me the beef if I ate it in our room so that none of the oldsters would see it and want it, too. He doesn't have enough of the beef to make it for more than a couple of servings."

"I'm almost jealous of your ability to get special dishes out of the chef, but since I have nothing to complain about, I'm just going to remind you to either put on a glamour or keep your cape handy. I'll be back before it's time to dress for the party."

"I would tell Paolo to bring an extra piece of the *gâteau au chocolat gianduja et la crème anglaise aux gousses de vanille bourbon*, but because you insist on treating me like a child, I may well forget to do so," she warned as I opened the door.

I did a little mental translating. "Enjoy your righteous indignation. I just hope the bourbon custard doesn't overwhelm the chocolate cake. Be good."

She gave an audible snort at that command, and picked up her book again. I headed off toward the lounge, where I would mingle with everyone, making sure they all saw me before we set off for the afternoon trip.

SEVEN

I watched the first of the two hired tour buses pull away from the train station with a profound sense of relief. I'd glimpsed Alan heading through the station with a group of other tourists, and assumed he had gone on the first bus.

"That gives me a few hours," I said, hurrying through the station back to where the Byzantine Express stood on a distant track, its blue-and-white cars glistening in the afternoon sun.

The staff was busy tidying up the interior while the bulk of the passengers were off on the excursion, although I noticed a few people were dotted about the lounge car, and two elderly men were patrolling up and down the platform, chatting while they got some exercise.

I skulked around until the attendant responsible for the sleeping car where Rennie and her husband were bunked left to carry off an armload of used towels. Luckily, she had left the compartments open while she moved through them cleaning, and I—after a couple of furtive glances up and down the passage—dashed into the one belonging to Rennie, quietly closing the door. "Right. Let's do this."

It didn't take me long to search the few things set in a day bag that sat on the table, or the items scattered in the mini washroom that was part of the compartment. I turned to face the garment bag hanging on the back of the door. "That just leaves you," I said, wondering if there was some certain way that Alan had left the bag zipped. It looked perfectly normal, but I took care to unzip it carefully, keeping an ear cocked for the sound of the returning steward.

The bag contained nothing but a few pairs of pants, a couple of shirts, a pair of men's dress shoes, and a stiff black object that I identified as a tuxedo. I rezipped the garment bag, glancing around the room while frowning. "That's Alan, but where are Rennie's—"

A noise from the hallway had me diving for the space under the seat. It was normally used for storing extra bags, and indeed, I found one there that I hurriedly squished myself behind, thanking the stars that I had enough polter blood that I could disappear into shadows.

The door opened and I caught a glimpse of the steward's shoes as she entered the cabin, obviously looking around before she clicked her tongue, and murmured something in German about becoming forgetful. She puttered around the room for a few minutes, replacing glasses in the washroom area, and putting a small basket of wrapped afternoon treats on the table before she left, about to close the door when Alan's voice sounded.

"Cleaning up, are you? I need to get my bag … no, the small toiletries bag, just there. Thank you."

I held my breath for the count of ten after they left, the steward closing the door softly behind her.

"That was way too close," I whispered to myself, squirming out from under the seat, brushing off the bits of lint and hair that had gathered under there before I pulled the soft canvas bag out and opened it.

"Bingo." A small phone was tucked into an inner pocket, and after powering it up, I opened up the contacts list, seeing an entry for Alan, but not one for Rennie. "So you're her phone. Good."

I hesitated for a second, then with a quick peek out the window, dug through the phone until I came to the media directory. There were two videos, although both were evidently filmed while the phone rested in a pocket or bag, because there was no visual, just muffled sound.

"—I'm not going to tolerate this!" a man's voice boomed out of it. With an oath and a worried glance at the closed door, I turned the volume way down. "You've tried your best to destroy me, but you lost. You aren't going to do this, Rennie. You should know by now that you won't win against me."

"It's you who is trying to kill me," a woman's voice said, throbbing with emotion. "Why do you hate me so? Why do you want me gone?"

"Do you think I'm stupid? I know exactly what you're doing, and I'm not going to stand for it. You won't win! Stop trying!" Alan sounded almost deranged, his voice rising with each word.

"I don't want to win. I just want to be at peace." Rennie's words were choked, leaving me feeling nauseous. I also felt like the worst sort of eavesdropper, but I had to know what the videos said, and Rennie had given me permission.

"Now I know you're mad," Alan all but snarled. "Your little stunt back there almost worked, but not quite. And you're crazy if you think I'm going to let you have a second chance."

The audio was filled with a faint buzzing noise; then a whisper sounded as if Rennie was holding the phone to her mouth. "He's going to try to kill me. He said he'd rig the airbag on our car and see to it that he survived a crash, but I didn't. I tried to escape, but he caught me, and forced me back."

That was followed by a gasp as footsteps sounded in the background; then the audio stopped. I had no problem picturing Rennie secretly recording the threat that Alan posed to her, and stopping when he found her.

I ground my teeth for a minute, fighting to control my anger. Then I tapped on the second video. It was shorter, just eight seconds, and like the other, the video itself was black, while the audio track consisted of odd grunting noises. That continued for seven seconds; then a man gasped and asked, "What the he—" before the video stopped.

"Clearly you walked in on Rennie trying to escape. Or find proof of your mistreatment," I told the phone before checking it for any other videos, but there were none. I was tempted to look at the photos, but Rennie hadn't given me permission to do so, so I figured I'd wait until I could get a word with her again, and ask if there was anything else on the phone we could use as proof of her abuse.

I made it out of the cabin and compartment before spotting anyone. I greeted the stewards, and the odd Mrs. Summerville, who had claimed her usual spot in the lounge car, before hurrying back to our suite, full of news to share with Pixie.

The compartment was empty. I frowned, then lowered the window and stuck my head out of it, wondering if she'd decided to take a stroll, but there was no sign of her on that platform.

Ten minutes later I'd searched the entirety of the train station, and returned to the train, asking Paolo if he'd seen Pixie.

"She did not go with the others?" he asked, shaking his head. "No, she was not in the suite a short while ago when I was in there."

"Thanks," I said, wondering what had happened to her.

He moved off to deal with the other two suites in our car, leaving me to pinch my lip as I thought.

There weren't many places she could get to on the train, and I didn't think she'd go wander around the town on her own. It's not like there was anything to attract her—a sudden horrible thought struck me, and I dashed off down the train, hunting through all the open cabins and restaurant cars, which were being cleaned, and scattered apologies behind me as I leaped over stewards vacuuming, setting up tables, and polishing the fixtures.

Nowhere did I see Pixie, or my secondary targets of Teodor and Olga. It was as if all three had disappeared off the train.

"I could see the last two stepping out for a change of scenery, but not Pixie," I growled to myself as I headed toward the sleeper cars at the other end of the train. "There's nothing out there nearly as enticing as what this train holds." I entered car H, and paused, the hairs on my arm standing with the static in the air.

"Oh, you are so in for it now—" I threw open the door to compartment five, and froze for a second.

Pixie was squashed up against the window, her face red, her eyes wide and unseeing but filled with terror, all four of her arms fighting the hand that gripped her by the neck so hard that its fingers were white.

It was a man who had her pinned up against the window, one with black hair slicked back in the style of a hundred years before, and in his right hand, he held high a glinting silver object. For one moment I thought it was a knife, but the second it started its downward arc toward Pixie, I realized it was a straightedge razor.

Before I could even think, my hands were drawing the symbols of banishment, and I was pulling on the power that surrounded all living things, charging up my abilities until just as the razor touched Pixie's neck, I blasted power outward, slamming it into the murderous spirit.

He spun around as the wave hit him, his face twisted with hate and fury, and then his form dissolved into nothing, a faint trickling of black sooty ash drifting slowly to the carpet.

I had Pixie before she could collapse, coughing and sputtering as I eased her onto the long bench seat that was found in the sleeper cars. She clutched at me with two hands while the other two waved around as she drew in great, shuddering hoarse breaths. "Didn't— jumped me—"

"Don't talk," I told her, kneeling before her to examine the thin line of blood that dribbled from the nick on her neck. "Just breathe. Give yourself time to recover."

"Herv—" She choked on the word.

"He's gone." I kept my hands on her knees, my gaze holding steady onto hers. "He can't hurt you now."

Tears made her eyes swim as she continued to suck in air, a few of them spilling over onto her cheeks. Angrily, she rubbed them away, her expression now an odd one of mingled defiance and gratitude. "I wasn't afraid," she finally said, her voice more a croak than anything else.

"You should be," I said, the adrenaline pumping through me finally starting to fade. "You should be utterly and completely terrified. Pixie, you could have been killed!"

"I didn't think he would hurt me. I just figured he'd yell a bit, and I could tell him to leave women alone because we're not responsible for him getting shot. I never thought he'd attack me. Deus! What was his problem?"

"I told you not to come here. I explicitly told you not to, and yet, you did anyway. And now look what's happened."

"I'm not hurt," she said, the defiance growing. She touched the spot on her neck. "Well, barely hurt. So it's not like anything horrible happened. If anything, it was good I came here, because now no one will have to be bothered by that asshat ghost."

A great shudder of fear, revulsion, and the aftereffects of adrenaline rippled through me. "And why is that?" I asked, closing my eyes for a moment against a wave of nausea.

"Because you zapped him out of here." She gave her neck a tentative rub, then grimaced. "I'll have to wear a long scarf around my neck tonight at the party. Luckily, I have one, and I don't think my lady adventurer will look odd wearing it. It's kind of dashing."

I dropped my head on my hands, which were still on her knees. "Goddess give me strength."

"For what?" Pixie asked, moving her legs a little.

I released her knees and hauled myself onto the seat next to her. "Repeat what you said before you mentioned the scarf."

"What?" Her face screwed up as she thought. "That it's good I came in here to confront Hervé?"

"After that."

"That you zapped him to Abaddon?" She gave a little shake of her head, one that implied I was acting like a drama queen.

"I didn't banish him to Abaddon. I can't do that. I can, however, transport spirits to the Akasha."

"Where they can't get out," she said, giving a nonchalant shrug. "So what's the diff?"

"The difference is this." I held out my wrist, jumping a little when I realized the monitor face, which normally appeared black, was now blinking with a big red ALERT across its face. If I had any hope that my actions would escape notice, that hope was now dead. "Shit. They know."

Her eyes widened, and she had the grace to look momentarily guilty. "Oh. Your thingie."

"My prohibition to perform any exterminations, yes. Which I just did in order to save you."

She sat silent for a few minutes, then gave a defiant toss of her head. "There were extenuating circumstances. They won't punish you because of that, right?"

"Wrong. I was specifically forbidden to banish spirits, and I violated that. Given the terms of my wergeld, I'm bound to follow the rules the Akashic League sets for me. This is serious, Pixie. Very serious."

She pursed her lips; then before I could act, she had the monitor off my wrist, and was dashing out of the compartment.

"Pixie …" I stopped, slumping against the back of the seat, too drained now that the adrenaline was gone.

A form shimmered into view. "We felt something," Teodor said, more translucent than not. He glanced around, his eyes wary. "This is Hervé's compartment."

"Yes. He's gone."

"Gone where?" Olga drifted through the door. "He

never leaves the train. We were in town, visiting some favorite places, when we felt … something …"

"What you felt was a removal of energy," I told them, and hoisted myself to my feet. "Strictly speaking, the energy that was Hervé."

"You banished him?" Olga's lips, now painted bright red, pursed for a moment as she slid Teodor an unreadable glance. "To the Akasha?"

"Yes, and yes, and before you ask, no, I did not intend to do so. In fact, I was forbidden to do anything of the sort, as I mentioned the other day." I rubbed my wrist where the monitor had been. "And I'm going to be in a world of trouble over it."

"Then why …" Teodor stopped, nodding. "Ah. He attacked you?"

"Pixie, not me. I wouldn't have come here to be put in a position to defend myself. And now Pixie is going who knows where to ditch my monitor, not that it will do any good to do so, but she's a bit impulsive at times." I thought for a minute, then admitted, "To be honest, I'd probably have done something like that when I was her age."

"What will you do?" Olga asked, ignoring an older couple who made their way down the corridor. I smiled when they shot me a not very friendly look, obviously aware that I was not the valid occupant of the compartment. They didn't seem to notice Olga and Teodor, which confirmed my thought that they were in a transitive state.

What was curious was that Pixie had seen them. I thought back to their visit to our suite, and tried to remember if they appeared corporeal after Pixie had arrived. I thought not. They certainly hadn't been when Paolo brought champagne.

I made a mental note to have a word with Pixie, and gave the pair of ghosts a feeble smile. "I'm going to continue the trip. I suspect I'll hear from the League shortly, and then I'll most likely have to appear before the Istanbul office."

They murmured some platitudes, but I wasn't really in the mood for polite chitchat about the mess that my life presently comprised, and instead returned glumly to the suite to lie down on the bed with a damp cloth over my eyes.

"OK, that's done." Pixie entered the room with a rush of air. "I parked your monitor inside a student's backpack, so if they are tracking you, they'll hang around town here while we go on. They'll never find you."

"Of course they'll find me. If nothing else, they'll send thief takers after me," I told her from under the washcloth.

I could feel her standing at the foot of my bed. "You have a migraine, or something?"

"No." I peeled up one edge of the cloth and peered balefully at her. "Just a normal, everyday four-alarm headache."

"What—" She stiffened, her expression turning mulish. "Deus! I didn't know it would get you in trouble, OK? You don't have to treat me like a criminal!"

"How on earth have I treated you like a criminal?" I pulled off the washcloth and sat up to look at her.

Her gaze dropped, and she moved restlessly around the compartment, flitting from chair to sofa to bathroom. "You're trying to make me feel guilty."

"If you feel guilty, that's on you," I told her, then sighed, and patted the bed next to me. Reluctantly, she slid onto the bottom edge. "Pixie, I'm not trying to guilt you. I'm also not treating you like a criminal, and if you feel that I am, then I'm sorry. I would like to know why you went to that compartment when I expressly forbade you to do so, however."

"I thought I could help, OK?" Her shoulders were drawn up, leaving her an obviously miserable ball of teen angst. "You always have to help people, and I thought it would be nice if someone helped you, instead. So I was going to go yell at that stupid ghost to lighten up already, but he … he …"

"He was manic," I said, nodding. "I could feel that energy from him."

"He said I had no right to be," she said softly, rubbing all of her arms.

"To be there?"

"To be, period. He said I was an abomination, and that I didn't deserve to live." It didn't seem possible, but she hunched over even more, her body language screaming unhappiness.

I sighed, and slid down the bed until I could wrap an arm around her. She remained stiff next to me, but didn't pull away. "You're not an abomination, but you know that. I'm sorry that Hervé attacked you. I wish I could have kept that from you, but I suppose, given that you weren't hurt, it was good for you to learn for yourself that not all spirits are friendly. Or even harmless."

"He was evil," she said softly.

"He was, but you aren't. I know that you meant well, Pixie."

She peeked at me through the corner of her eye. "You're mad at me, though."

"Of course I'm angry. I asked you not to do something, and you chose to disregard that request."

"It was more of an order," she said with another shrug.

"And you don't like orders, but you have to understand that when it comes to all things spirits, then I usually have the experience to back up the reason for the orders. So next time, please heed me."

"Will you get in a lot of trouble?" she asked.

"Probably some trouble. Just how much depends on whether or not the people in the Istanbul branch are understanding of the situation." I gave her a quick squeeze, and for a few seconds, she relaxed into me. "But I'm hoping that the fact that the spirit has a long history of violence, not to mention he was close to slitting your throat, buys me a little grace."

My phone, which had been chirping to indicate incoming texts, finally burst into a song that meant someone was calling.

"Aren't you going to answer that?" Pixie asked, scooting a foot away.

"I'd really rather not," I said, wanting to sigh again, but I had a feeling I'd been doing too much sighing of late. Instead, I pulled out my phone and grimaced at the name displayed before answering.

"This is Guy de Bartoille at the Pacific Northwest Akashic League office. We have a report of your TAE monitor being activated," an impersonal man's voice said. "Can you confirm the accuracy of the alarm?"

"Yes," I said, lying back down on the bed to stare at the fancy woodwork on the train car ceiling. "It went off."

"And the reason that it went off was because you conducted some form of transmortis anomaly extermination event?" Guy asked.

"Yup." I decided that I'd leave explanations for whatever local official with whom I was bound to speak.

"I see. And can you verify that you are at the moment on the way to the nearest Akashic League office to surrender yourself? I see by the tracking information on the monitor that you are presently in Siófok, Hungary. That means the nearest League office can be found in Budapest. Can you confirm that you are en route to that location?"

"I am on the way to Budapest," I said, one arm over my eyes. I wondered if the League was going to toss me in the Akasha with all the spirits I'd banished there, and what would happen to Pixie, Adam, and my father—not to mention all the imps, and my spirits—if I was thrown into it without any chance of return.

My stomach felt like it was filled with cement.

"I will so note your statement, and will inform the Budapest office to expect you within the next twenty-four hours."

"Yeah, that's not going to happen." The words were out before I realized they came from my mouth. I pulled my arm from where it hid my eyes, and stared with surprise at an equally surprised Pixie, who now stood next to the bed.

"I beg your pardon?" Guy asked, his tone still impersonal and polite.

"I said I wouldn't be going to the Budapest office. My trip ends in Istanbul. Until that point, I can't leave my charge, Pixie O'Hara."

"Akashic League rules state—"

"And the Home for Innocents rules supersede League rules when it comes to the safety and welfare of minors," I interrupted, making a face at Pixie that expressed just how idiotic I felt arguing. She made a little fist pump in response. "And I will not leave my ward unprotected on a train filled with strangers. Once we arrive in Istanbul, then I will speak with the people at the Akashic League. But until then, no."

"I'm afraid you have no choice about this, Ms. Marx," Guy said, a note of steel entering his voice. "You must turn yourself in to the nearest facility for the violation of your terms of employment. There are no exceptions allowed in this situation. The laws governing the League are most clear about this."

"You can take your laws and shove them where the sun don't shine," I said, sitting up, smiling when Pixie gave a silent whoop and twirled around in a jig of celebration. "Because I am just not doing it, OK? Tell the Istanbul office I'll be there in two days."

"I regret to inform you that a refusal to acknowledge the authority of the Akashic League will result in your apprehension by authorized individuals of the L'au-dela."

"You can send thief takers after me if you like, but I suspect they'll have a hard time getting on the train, since it's full of very rich people who don't like to be disturbed. Besides, I said I'll be in Istanbul in two days. That's all you're getting from me."

"I have so noted your statement," Guy said, his voice expressing nothing but a mild sense of disappointment. "I'm afraid that it changes nothing, however."

"Then we have no reason to keep chatting, do we? Goodbye." And before Guy could do more than take a breath preparatory to speaking, I hung up. Then after quickly checking my texts—five of which were from the local League office demanding that I call them immediately—I turned off my phone altogether.

"That was badass," Pixie said, applauding lightly when I stood up. "Man, they're going to be so pissed at you."

"Yes, they are." I fixed her with a look that I hoped expressed much.

She stopped celebrating, and resumed her defiant stance. "You'll explain it to the people in Turkey, though. So there's no need to worry, right?"

"I don't know," I told her, feeling like she needed to hear the truth. "I don't know what they'll do, but at least my refusal to turn myself in at Budapest gives me two days to try to work up a case for why they shouldn't toss my butt into the Akasha."

She sobered up after that, and we spent the next hour in quiet while I lay on the bed, wishing I were anywhere but there, that Adam were here, and, finally, that the League would just get off my back.

I must have dozed off, because when I woke up, the train was in motion again, and Pixie was not in the compartment.

I found her sitting with Rev and Donna, her phone in hand, glamour in place, and wearing the peacock-blue lounging pajamas.

"There's Karma," Donna said, waving a martini glass at me. "How do you feel? Your niece said you had a headache and were sleeping. You missed the most delightful detective. He taught us so many things about how to determine a murderer, didn't he?"

"He was OK. Nothing to write home about. I've seen better guys on the detective cable channel, but I suppose not everyone can be that level of good," Pixie said, looking up from her phone. She gave me a quick, piercing glance that asked a question. I gave her a little nod to let her know I was all right, then offered a smile to Donna and Rev.

"I'm sorry to have missed the detective, but my head feels much better for the nap." I sat down on one of the chairs that faced Rev, and waved away a passing attendant who asked if I desired a beverage. "Where are we?

I've lost track of where we're supposed to be, other than I know we'll be pulling in to Budapest shortly before the mystery party starts."

"We're about a half hour away from Budapest," Rev answered, glancing at his watch. "The party starts at eight. … It's six now. … Yes, I believe that will leave a little time to stretch my legs at the station once we get there."

"Is it a particularly nice station?" I asked, wondering if there was something we should see, or if time would be better spent in decking ourselves out for the party.

"Oh, Keleti station is quite lovely," Donna said quickly, handing off her empty glass and asking for another one. "It's one of those grand Victorian structures, you know, but very eclectic. There are some frescoes inside that I love seeing when I'm in Budapest, so if you have the time, I urge you to take a few pictures."

"According to my literature," Rev said, pulling out a tourist pamphlet, "there are a variety of shops, cafés, and a supermarket. I don't know about you, but I plan to see what sort of toothpaste is used in Hungary. Collecting toothpastes of other countries is a little hobby of mine," he said in a confidential tone to Pixie, who looked at him with a mild expression of disbelief.

"I'll have to check out the frescoes if the train is going to stop long enough." I was about to pull out my phone to check the schedule of stops, but Donna, sipping on her fresh drink, waved and yoo-hooed as her sisters entered the lounge, standing up as she said, "We're there for an hour, I believe. Allison, what on earth are you wearing? Girl, not only is it not time to dress for the murder mystery—that's Edwardian, not Roaring Twenties. For heaven's sake …" She hustled her sister off before the latter had the chance to do more than protest that she thought it was pretty.

June, the third sister, snagged Donna's martini as she passed, and immediately sat down with a chatty group of Canadian tourists.

"I've heard all about Amelia, the lady anthropologist," Rev said, sipping at what looked like a cranberry tonic. "But what of you?"

"Lady archaeologist," Pixie corrected.

"Alas, I'm nowhere as dashing as the lady adventurer. My role is that of Mary, downtrodden maid to the demanding Lady Waverly. Speaking of which, do you know who is playing her? I should probably chat with her so she knows I'll be her lackey for the evening."

"What does a lackey do?" Pixie asked, glancing up from her phone.

"Fetch shawls and smelling salts, walk small lapdogs, adjust pillows, move screens to prevent drafts," I said, waving a wan hand. "That sort of thing."

"So, like a slave," she said, returning her attention to her phone. "I'd much rather be a dashing archaeologist battling mummies and curses and thirst trap rich dudes funding the digs."

"Mrs. Summerville, I believe, is to be Lady Waverly," Rev said.

My shoulders slumped at that. I didn't mind the woman so much, but she was a bit overpowering, and I had a feeling she would take all too well to a role that had me running around for her.

Just as I was going to make a comment about my costume, a faint breeze behind me tickled my neck, sending a shiver down my spine.

Suddenly, Alan Taylor was at my side, his hand on my arm as he more or less pulled me to my feet. "A word with you, Mrs. Marx, if you please."

I opened my mouth to protest, but he was already hustling me down the length of the car, and out into the velvet-cloth-covered connector area, which was empty of everyone.

"What the hell do you think you're doing?" I asked, jerking my arm from him when he spun me around to face him. "I do not take kindly to be handled in such a manner."

"I don't give a damn what you take kindly to," he said in a near snarl. His expression was as black as a thundercloud, his eyes glittering dangerously. "I know what you are. I'm not blind or clueless. I know what you're trying to do. She's trying to get a hold of my business, isn't she? She's always wanted it. I have no doubt that's why she married me. What a fool I was, falling for her act, believing the lies that fell from her lips. Well, you can tell her that it's not going to work. She tried and failed, and now there's nothing she can do. So tell her that, and keep your nose out of my business."

The threat in his voice was palpable. I took a step back, my heart beating so loudly all I could hear was the sound of it in my ears.

"I don't know—" I started to say, fearing that somehow he'd gotten the truth out of Rennie, and had punished her.

Alan all but snarled an oath. "Do I make myself clear? Just stay away from me!"

Pixie appeared through the doorway, her gaze watchful.

"I don't particularly want to have anything to do with you," I told Alan Taylor. "Your wife, however, is a different matter."

He leaned forward, his eyes narrowed on me, forcing me to take two more steps back. "If you continue down the path of helping Rennie, you'll be sorry. So sorry."

I opened my mouth to protest, but he brushed past me, heading toward the sleeping cars.

"Well, that's that," I said somewhat shakily when Pixie moved over next to me, both of us watching as Alan disappeared into the next car. "He obviously knows what I'm here for. I just hope Rennie is all right."

"We can go flicker at him," Pixie suggested. "Maybe drug him somehow? I have the sleeping pills that Dr. Wellbottom gave me."

"No to the drugging, and I don't think he's going to be scared by polters," I said slowly, rubbing my arm where he'd held me so tightly.

"We can be really freaky when we want," she said. "But maybe there's something else we could do. What do you think would scare the crap out of him?"

"The truth," I said slowly, and, taking a deep breath, turned to go to our own car. "And I'm going to see to it that it comes out."

EIGHT

An hour later we headed back toward the train after having spent a little time exploring the station, seeing the murals and the great window at the entrance and, more important in Pixie's mind, visiting as many shops as she could in the half hour I gave her.

"We may not need a full hour to get dressed for the party, but I'd rather be safe than—holy shitsnacks!"

We emerged onto the platform where our train was parked, several other members of the journey either milling around outside or slowly drifting their way back from visiting the station, but ahead of me, I saw the back of a man who was standing next to one of the attendants. The size of him, the set of the shoulder, the slightly curly brown hair—it was all oddly familiar, and wholly out of place.

The man must have heard me because he turned his head, and smiled.

"Oooh," Pixie said, her eyebrows rising, casting me a speculative look.

"Adam!" I said, delighted, unable to keep from smiling broadly and almost running toward him. I didn't exactly throw myself into his arms, but it was a near thing, and I most definitely did hug him, and even managed to press an awkward kiss to one corner of his mouth.

"There you are. The attendant here said you two went off to do some shopping."

"What on earth are you doing here? I thought you were at the trial?" A horrible thought struck me, and I said softly, "Oh goddess. You're here to arrest me, aren't you?"

"No," he said slowly, his eyes narrowing. "Why would you ask that? Oh lord. You haven't killed someone else, have you?"

Pixie snorted a laugh as I whomped Adam on the arm. "Of course I haven't! It's just … er … I wasn't expecting you."

"Mm-hmm." He kept an arm around me even as he gave me a long look, but instead of conducting a third degree as I expected, he said, "I was tied up until a mistrial was declared because two of the jurors were caught taking paybacks from the defendants. Hello, Pixie. Have you been having a good trip?"

"Eh," she said, waggling her hand. "It's OK. Karma has been doing the drama thing, but you know how that goes."

Adam released me and held open his arms. Pixie made a face but, after ten seconds' thought, finally heaved a dramatic sigh and stood bolt upright with her arms stiffly at her side, wearing the most martyred of expressions. Adam gave her a quick hug, then, with a hand on my waist, turned back to the train.

"I'm sure Karma couldn't possibly indulge in any drama, certainly not the kind that would cause her to greet someone with a query regarding a possible arrest. And to answer the question that I know you want to ask, Karma, I'm hoping to spend what time I have with you. Assuming the offer to travel to Istanbul still stands?"

There was a morsel of doubt in his clear blue eyes, but I smiled, and gave him a quick hug before shooing Pixie onto the train. "Of course. There's plenty of room, and I told Paolo that you might be joining us if you could, although since I haven't heard from you, I figured that was off the table."

"He's going to stay with us?" Pixie asked once we got to the suite, and Adam, who had only a small bag with him, gawked in outright amazement at our accommodation. "Ew! I don't want to hear you guys having sex!"

"The door, as you know well because I close it every time I go to bed or change my clothes, does in fact close completely. But regardless of that, the living arrangements are a bit too … tight … to indulge in anything but snoozing. I promise I won't do anything more than hold his hand, all right?"

She looked faintly disgusted, but said, "OK, but I'm going to hold you to that. If you guys forget, I'll tell Dr. Wellbottom," before flopping down onto the sofa. Adam was inspecting one of the marquetry panels, whistling softly to himself.

"Deal," I said, watching Adam. Just the sight of him made me feel like a tight band across my chest had been loosened. I nudged Adam's arm when he had moved on to the drinks cabinet. "Hello? I'm beginning to think you joined us just for this glorious suite and not for the company inside of it."

"To be fair, I can see you back home," he said, pulling the blown-glass stopper off a decanter, and sniffing at the contents (whiskey). A blissful look crept over his face. "But this is something else—ow!"

"You deserve that pinch," I said, nodding toward the cabinet. "Pour us each one of those, will you? After the day I've had, I definitely need one. And no, you don't need any whiskey. You can have one glass of champagne at the party, or ginger beer, but no hard spirits."

The last was spoken to Pixie, who wrinkled her nose. "Dude! I don't even like whiskey. It's too rubbing alcohol for me."

Adam murmured something that sounded like "Philistine," but handed me a glass and took a seat in the chair.

I sipped the drink while he brought us up to date as to the happenings at the trial, and then how Dad had encouraged him to join us.

"Subtle, very subtle, Dad," I murmured, calling, "Come in," when someone knocked at the door.

Paolo entered with a clipboard, and we spent the next ten minutes getting Adam situated. Luckily, the company was understanding when I explained he'd been unable to join us at the beginning of the trip.

"That reminds me, what are you going to do for the party tonight?" I asked when Paolo took his leave with Adam's passport and visa for Turkey.

Adam looked a bit disconcerted. "Are you sure it's all right for that man to just walk off with my passport like that? There's such a thing as the trade in stolen identity documents."

"Yes, it's what they do. The stewards hold all the docs so that when we go into a new country, they can show the officials, and we won't be woken up in the middle of the night. They'll give them back once we're in Istanbul, and you can ask for them if you need it at a stop. Crap, I forgot to give him back mine. I changed some money at the train station and had to show my passport. I'll have to remember to give it to him later. Costume?"

"Hmm?" He didn't look happy at the loss of his passport but, after I showed him where he could stow his suitcase, returned to our little sitting room. "Oh, I'm going as an Interpol agent. I brought a suit."

"Speaking of which, I suppose we should start to get ready. Pixie, you can use my room to change if you want."

"OK, but if I open the door and find Adam kissing you, I'm going to have major trauma and will probably puke all over the place." She took her garment bag into my bedroom, making sure to slam shut the door.

Adam looked thoughtfully at the intricate door. "It's good to see her warming up to me. So, you want to tell me about this drama that had you expecting to be arrested?"

"Oh, goddess, no. Yes. Do I have to?" I slumped down on the sofa in exactly the same manner Pixie used at her most petulant. "Can't we talk about something more pleasant, instead? Like, how you flew halfway around the world to be with us, and how you're doing, and whether or not I can touch your chest, and exactly how you expect me to get through the next two days if we can't do things in private that I really want to do?"

"That was meaty," he said, sitting next to me, and, to my extreme pleasure, pulled me up against his side. I let myself lean into him, melting into him at the sensation of his solid warmth. "There was a lot packed into a few sentences. Let's take them one by one, shall we?"

"You're such a cop," I said, closing my eyes and ignoring my burdens for a few seconds.

"Marshal, and why do I have the feeling that you're not just a bit frazzled from having to be with Pixie in close confines for several days, but you're actively attempting to distract me from something unpleasant? Is it the sort of unpleasant that I'm going to find problematic, Karma?"

I decided I was due a mental sigh at the note of resignation in his voice, and opened my eyes, patted his leg, then moved over to the chair facing him. "Yes, very problematic. You remember how my boss put new restrictions on what I could and couldn't do?"

His chocolate-brown brows pulled together, then flattened out when his gaze took in my bare wrist. "You don't appear to be wearing the monitor the Akashic League gave you. Where is it?"

"Traveling around a town in Hungary in the backpack of a student, if what Pixie told me is true, and I have no reason to doubt her. She seldom outright lies."

"What did you do?" he asked, his shoulders sagging a little.

"Your ability to cut right to the point is one of those things that I like about you," I said, my emotions tangled. I was simultaneously exhausted, wired and aroused at his nearness, and worried about not only Rennie, but what was going to happen to me when I turned myself in at Istanbul. "Although I could do without the Saint Adam the Martyred expression. If anything, I should be the one looking like the world was dumping on me. Which it is."

"What did you do?" he repeated.

"I banished a ghost." I shot a glance at the closed door to my bedroom and quickly told Adam about Hervé.

His frown was prodigious by the time I was finished, and he was pacing up and down the length of our compartment, one hand rubbing his chin. "This is serious, Karma. If the Akashic League has called for your capture, then that puts me in a very difficult situation. Technically, as a member of the Watch, I would need to take you into custody."

"I had a horrible feeling that was going to be what you'd say," I said, diving headlong into a pity party. "But I don't know for a fact that they've unleashed thief takers. I told them several times I would be going to the League office in Istanbul. Surely it has to be easier for them to simply let me do that than hire someone who then has to smuggle himself on the train, because I can tell you that the train people take very good care that only ticket holders get on board. That's one of the side effects of having a bunch of rich people along for the ride."

"The fact still remains that you are in violation of the terms of your wergeld with the League," he pointed out.

"Yes, but that's League business, nothing to do with the Watch."

He rubbed his chin some more. "I suppose that's true, although my boss will have my balls on a platter if he finds out that there was a warrant for your arrest and I did nothing about it."

I lifted my hands and let them fall in an expression of sheer, unadulterated helplessness. "I can't guarantee they haven't, but it doesn't seem likely. The League knows me. They have me on two wergeld charges. I have Pixie. They know I'm not going to go rogue and hide."

"True." He paced a bit more. "As for the charge itself … the extermination on its own would be no problem. You are a licensed TAE, and the spirit attacked Pixie. I'm not a legal expert, but I can't help but think that the League would take that into account when reviewing the act of you breaking the prohibitions of your service."

"I was hoping that the fact that Pixie is technically a child and would have died had Hervé not been stopped would buy me a little grace." I eyed the whiskey decanter, but decided that getting sloshed wouldn't do any good.

"It makes sense to me, but as I said, I'm no lawyer." He stopped in front of me, all six feet four inches of a man so delicious that my mind and body were willing to forget the dire peril in which I found myself just in case I wanted to romp all over him.

"What are you going to do?" I asked, still miserably ensconced in my pity party.

"About telling the Watch where you are?"

I nodded.

He was silent for almost a minute before he said, "Nothing until Istanbul, when I'll accompany you to the League office. I don't know for a fact that a warrant has been issued for your arrest, so I can't be expected to act in an official capacity. I will be happy to act as a character witness for you to the Akashic League people, assuming you don't have any contacts in this area of Europe."

"I don't, and I'd be grateful for any help you want to give."

Pixie swung open the door in a dramatic fashion, and struck a pose. To my surprise, she wasn't wearing the expected jodhpurs and coat ensemble, but instead had on a handkerchief-hem, calf-length copper-colored dress with a crossed bodice and beautiful beading.

"What happened to your archaeologist outfit?" I asked, admiring the dress nonetheless. It was truly gorgeous, and made me resent my own meager costume.

She gave a little toss of her head. She had the glamour in place, so she was back to sporting a sleek black bob à la Louise Brooks. "I was reading a blog this afternoon, and it talked about white colonialism, and how promoting that is hurtful to the Egyptian people of the time. So instead of wearing something that promotes how white society stomped in and took over all the digs, I am representing a European woman who values all cultures. My lady archaeologist has given up her dig to a local man, and is instead helping him. She also attends dances, and secures investments for the dig by turning the heads of the wealthy European and American men."

"That's quite a backstory," Adam said, nodding his head. "My grandmother is Egyptian, and I think she'd appreciate you acknowledging the colonization of Egypt."

"Do you have pictures of what she wore in the 1920s?" Pixie asked, moving over to stand next to Adam when he pulled out his phone.

"I do back home, but none here, although this is the latest photo I have of her." Pixie and I admired the dark-haired woman who had the same mischievous glint to her eye that I saw in Adam. "I'll have to hunt around for the old photo albums when we get back home."

Adam and Pixie chatted for the fifteen minutes it took me to get into my drab maid's costume, complete with heavily gelled hair that I scraped back into a bun on the back of my head. I added a pair of round metal glasses and, finally, pinned on a white maid's apron to the front of my nearly ankle-length black dress.

"You look like a cross between a Nazi and a sickly seal," I told my reflection. I had resisted the urge to add a wart to my nose, although I had used some of Pixie's cosmetics to enhance the already dark circles under my eyes.

"Wow, that really is horrible," Pixie said, walking in a circle around me.

"Thank you," I said, making a face at Adam. He stood with an indescribable expression, his gaze shifting between the shapeless dress and my slicked-back hair. "Er …"

"Yes, I'm supposed to look this way," I told him, relieving him from trying to summon a compliment about an obviously unattractive outfit. "I'm the poor, downtrodden maid. I figured I'd better look the part if Mrs. Summerville intends on enacting her role. And I'm fairly certain she will."

"Who?"

"One of the passengers. She's very grande dame, and has a dead parrot with her."

Adam blinked twice, then nodded. His ability to cope with unexpected and frequently outrageous bits of information was one of the things I most admired about him. "Right. I'll go change."

"I'd offer to help you, but I suspect Pixie would have a fit," I said with a wink at Pixie.

"Ew!" she said, which just made me laugh. I waited until Adam closed the door before asking her, "Does it really bother you to have Adam staying with us? You didn't seem to mind when we mentioned it back home, so I thought we were all right on that front."

She twitched a shoulder, but after a minute's silence, said, "No. Adam's OK. But …" She stopped.

"I understand. It's different when we're at home than all being squished together so tight here. Well, you can relax. I promise we won't do anything that will make you uncomfortable."

She rolled her eyes and murmured something about not treating her like a child, but I could tell that she was relieved, nonetheless.

A short while later an announcement came over the train's PA system that the gathering was underway in the lounge car, and that all participants of the murder mystery were requested to attend.

"I didn't know there was an option to just watch," I said, a little annoyed as I twitched my shabby dress before we headed out. "I would have done that if I'd known that."

"This is more fun. You get to catch a murderer."

"I've caught one. I can do without going through that again," I said with a glance back at Adam.

Heat flared in my cheeks when I caught him ogling my butt. His eyes snapped up to mine when he realized he was busted. His lips twitched.

I winked, and we followed along with everyone else to the lounge car. I was curious to see whether Alan Taylor was going to be present, and made a mental note to fill in Adam later as to what the former had said.

One of the rail line officials was acting as emcee, and as soon as everyone had gathered, and was possessed of a glass of champagne, he went over the history of the train and its tie to Agatha Christie, and proceeded to spin a story about a group of people gathered together to punish a man who had been suspected in the disappearance of a bride. It was exactly what I expected it to be, and I couldn't help but be intrigued.

"Any clue as to who the murderer is?" I asked Pixie in a whisper. The three of us were squished together on a love seat, with me in the middle, greatly enjoying being pressed so tightly against Adam.

"Rev," Pixie said quickly, nodding to the man in

question, who was dressed in the most impeccable white tuxedo I'd ever had the pleasure to see. "He's Mr. Foster, debonair New York tycoon, and has had four wives already. He's after Lady Waverly, I'm sure."

I slid Mrs. Summerville a look. She, like almost everyone present, had thrown herself into the costuming aspect of the evening's event, and was wearing a magnificent outfit of beaded peach-and-cream dress, a matching headband, and a couple of ostrich feathers that were so tall they brushed the top of the carriage when she stood. Her bird was clipped to a small evening bag, and hung at a drunken angle every time she gestured with the bag. "I have no doubt. She has to be rich if she can afford downtrodden maids."

"Yeah, but he's also clearly got some skeletons in the closet. I bet he's the one who killed the young bride of the Turkish ambassador."

"Who is the Turkish ambassador?" I asked, glancing around.

"Donna Spenser," Pixie answered.

Adam asked what we were whispering about, so I filled him in on Pixie's deductions.

"It's the ambassador," he stated.

"How do you know that? You haven't even met Donna."

He shrugged. "Diplomatic immunity."

"That, or it's you." Pixie slid me a look that had me sending it right back to her.

"We won't know until after dinner, will we?" was all I said, paying attention when the emcee briefly went through our alter egos, introducing each of us in turn, and giving a brief back story. Following that, we were given programs with notepads, and told to talk amongst ourselves for half an hour.

Alan Taylor had appeared by then, I noticed. But without his wife.

"You may work in pairs if you desire," the emcee added in a heavy French accent, "but in those situations, the prizes will be shared by both parties."

"You guys are going to pair up, I guess," Pixie said, shooting Adam a scathing look.

"Actually," I said, coming to a snap decision, my gaze on Alan Taylor at the opposite end of the car. I badly wanted to talk to him, but more important, Pixie was trying very hard to behave on this trip, and Hervé aside, she had done so. The last thing I wanted to do was foster the idea that once Adam was around, I lost interest in her. "I was going to suggest that you guys tackle the suspects together. I can buddy up with either Rev or Donna, or, goddess help me, Mrs. Summerville."

Pixie perked up, but immediately adopted a laissez-faire attitude. "I don't care," she said with a shrug, looking away from us. "It's fine if you guys want to be together."

I cocked an eyebrow at Adam, who took the suggestion in stride without so much as a sigh. I mouthed a thank-you at him when he said, "That works for me, since it will keep Karma elsewhere, so I won't be tempted to kiss her."

"Ugh," Pixie said, standing up and tugging on Adam's arm. "I think I liked it better when you wanted to kill us, Adam."

"I never wanted to kill you, just get you out of my house," he protested, and allowed himself to be led away.

I spent a few minutes with notebook in hand as I chatted with people, working my way down the car, keeping my eyes on Alan Taylor. He remained on the opposite end, apparently having a good time.

"And just where is your wife?" I asked softly to myself, wondering if I had time to make my way to his end of the lounge before we had to move to the next stage of the party.

"Dead, as you well know, since you're the one who found her." I spun around at the artificially deep voice. Donna stood behind me, having adopted a vaguely European accent. "Now, then, I believe I'm supposed to ask you some questions."

I glanced around and forcibly scooted her back to the passageway.

"What—uh—" she started to say in her normal voice, looking startled.

"Toilet paper stuck to your shoe," I whispered, and turned my back to block anyone as she hurriedly picked off the offending object and dashed into the nearby bathroom.

"Good lord, that would have been the death of me," she said with a breathy giggle as she returned, giving me a pat on the arm. "Thank you for catching that. Wait, I don't have any coming off my pants, do I?" She spun around and pulled the split tail of her tuxedo apart.

"Nope, everything is fine there."

"Whew. OK. Where were we?" She glanced past me at a high-pitched laugh. "Oh lord, Allison has had too much Bolly. Right. I'd better do this fast so I can keep her from making an exhibition of herself." She cleared her throat and said in her accented voice, "What do you know of Lady Waverly's dead daughter, my beloved bride of twenty minutes?"

I checked the fact sheet I was given. "Nothing other than she was very excited to be marrying you."

"You were her maid before you took a position with Lady Waverly, is that not right?"

"Yes," I said, and made a little bob, because I felt like it suited the persona of a drab maid. "Your bride was a dear, sweet girl who had no enemies in the world. Except the man who sullied her name when she was a shy and innocent young girl of eighteen. But about that, I cannot speak."

"Wow, you're good," Donna said, smiling conspiratorially. "Now it's your turn."

"I only have one question to ask people, I'm afraid, and that's where you were at ten p.m. the night of the disappearance."

Donna twiddled a bushy black mustache that promptly fell off and stuck to the toe of her shoe. She snatched it up, and held it on to her face with a finger. "I was in my carriage, awaiting the arrival of my blushing bride, and not, as some may tell you, in the carriage of another woman. Especially not a woman of the world who possessed a scarlet-and-gold dressing gown."

I noted her answer, and she, after a few more giggles, moved off to grace the nearest group of people with her ambassadorial self.

People were milling all around the lounge car, some seated, some standing, but nowhere did I see Rennie. Her husband, however, remained at the opposite end of the car, dressed, like Adam, in a dark suit. I had no idea what role he had, but since he appeared to be consulting his phone a lot, I wondered if he wasn't as into the party as he first appeared.

After a quick glance around the car, I slipped out, hesitating at the communal bathroom, then decided to use the one in my suite. I had to pass Alan's compartment to get there and, after another glance up and down the corridor, opened the door to peer in, hoping that Rennie would be there.

The compartment was empty. I peered around and narrowed my eyes on the bags, tempted to search them again in case Alan had hidden something incriminating, but I decided it wasn't worth risking being caught.

Ten minutes later when I returned to the lounge car, the emcee was speaking.

"—hope you have had ample time to search for clues and pinpoint false alibis," he said, beaming at us all. I moved over to where Adam stood next to Pixie. The former looked back at me with a question in his eyes.

"Had to use the bathroom," I whispered truthfully, since I had stopped by our suite.

"We will now progress with dinner, to be served simultaneously in two of the dining cars, after which our very own Detective Matisse D'Or will help you solve the disappearance of the Turkish ambassador's bride." The emcee gestured toward the doors, and helped the more frail up out of the low, comfy seats.

There was a general rush toward the restaurant cars, and I managed to pass close enough by Alan Taylor that I could say softly to him, "What have you done with your wife, Mr. Taylor?"

He turned narrowed eyes on me, sputtering, "You damned fool! I warned you not to interfere."

Adam was behind me, and rather than have it out right there, I continued on, but I made sure that we claimed a table at the far end so I could keep my eye on my red-haired adversary.

NINE

Dinner was as decadent as all the other meals had been.

"The menu is in French," Pixie informed Adam when we claimed our table. Luckily, we were able to take one for four people, and it gave me a good view of the entire restaurant car. "They can give you one with English if you want, but Paolo says that's rude, and people should learn more than just English."

"As it happens," Adam said, accepting a menu when the waiter handed them to us, "I speak French. As well as German, Russian, and a smattering of Arabic. Ah. *L'éventail de filets de bar et de rouget sur une fondue de fenouil.* I don't know that I've had red mullet before, but I like fennel."

I consulted the menu. "Is *le carré d'agneau pré-salé rôti dans une croûte aux fines herbes et la tuile de chorizo doux* lamb? It looks like lamb."

"Herb-crusted Mont-Saint-Michel rack of lamb with crunchy chorizo petal," Adam translated.

"Ew. We don't like lamb," Pixie said.

"We can skip that course, and just eat the fish and the stuffed sweet red peppers and eggplant," I told her.

"Le cornet de piquillos au boulgour et le panaché de courgettes, d'aubergines, et d'échalotes confites," she murmured.

"Show-off," I told her, smiling to take the sting out of the words. "I knew I should have taken French instead of Spanish at college."

"What is an Amalfi soft lemon cake?" Adam asked, still reading the menu.

"A cake. Lemony. And soft," I answered, my eyes on Alan Taylor when he rose from where he was sitting with an English couple. He spoke for a moment with the waiter, then left the carriage. "With some sort of vanilla cream."

"So I gathered from the description. I'm just trying to decide if I want that, or a *sélection du maître fromager.*"

Pixie's amused gaze met mine. We had a running joke about the master of cheeses being the best title of all the staff.

We ordered, accepted the obligatory glass of champagne, Pixie being especially casual as she sipped at her glass, and immediately tucked into a shrimp and caviar appetizer that was so artistically created, even I had to take a picture of it. Pixie was in ecstasies over it.

While she was taking pictures from several angles, Adam leaned close and whispered in my ear, "Do you want to tell me who it is you're watching for? Do I have a rival?"

I turned to look in surprise, rubbing my ear where his breath had tickled it. "How on earth—man, I'm going to regret dating a cop."

"Marshal," he corrected yet again, cocking an inquisitorial eyebrow.

"Alan Taylor," I whispered back.

"The man with the wife you were worried about?"

"Yes." I glanced at Pixie. I wasn't sure if I wanted her to know the path of my thoughts regarding Rennie and Alan.

"OK, you guys are going to, like, completely put me off my caviar if you keep whispering to each other," she said, tucking her phone back into her evening bag.

"Sheesh," I said, stabbing my fork into the perfectly grilled shrimp. "Can't kiss Adam, can't get jiggy in the dining car. The next time you call me bossy, I'm going to tell you to look in the mirror."

"Jiggy?" Pixie asked in horror at the same time that Adam, who was taking a sip of champagne, choked and sputtered into his napkin. "Deus, Karma! Do I even want to know what 'jiggy' is?"

"No. You're too young," I told her, helpfully patting Adam on the back until he stopped choking. "Actually, we weren't whispering sweet nothings to each other, so you can stop mentally writing a complaint about inappropriate behavior to be lodged with the Home for Innocents. Adam asked me who I was watching."

"Oh." She waved her fork as she ate her appetizer. "That's probably Rennie or Alan Taylor."

"The latter, and he left before eating," I said, my eyes on the door again. "I wonder why."

"Maybe he wanted to eat in his compartment with Rennie," she suggested.

"Rennie's not there," I said slowly, putting down my fork. I could feel Adam giving me a look, but I couldn't seem to tear my gaze from the far end of the dining car. "I checked earlier. I haven't seen her in some time, in fact. I can't help but wonder if she's here anymore."

Pixie's eyes grew round, her fork loaded with arugula, shrimp, and caviar paused midway to her mouth. "You think that Alan Taylor killed her and tossed her off the train, just like in the Agatha Christie I read this morning? Oh my god, he so could have done that when everyone was at Lake Balaton!"

"With everyone looking? I don't think so," I said, slowly shaking my head. "I'm trying to remember the last time I saw her."

"I saw her in the corridor before we got to Lake Balaton," Pixie said, chewing with a blissful expression.

I stared at her for a few seconds, then shot Adam a look, but he was scanning the people in the restaurant car and missed it. I knew that as a member of the Watch—and US Marshals—he tended to be hypervigilant in unfamiliar situations, but it still amazed me, since I didn't have nearly his ability to focus. "How much before Lake Balaton?"

"A couple of hours earlier." She frowned at her water glass, then gave a sharp nod. "Yeah, it was after lunch. I thought she was going to the bathroom, but she passed it and went into the next car, but when I followed, she disappeared. Must have gone into someone else's cabin. Or maybe that's when Alan Taylor murdered her and threw her off the train."

"No, I saw her after that. Right before we got into the station at Lake Balaton."

"OK, so that's when he offed her and dumped her."

"He wouldn't have had time," I said, trying to fit puzzle pieces together in my head.

"Could he have dumped her once we got into the station? Maybe her body was under the train, and no one saw her?" Pixie suggested.

Adam shook his head before I could answer. "Not likely. The body would have been discovered as soon as the train left, and the mortal officials would have contacted the train and had it stopped at the next station."

"Oh. That sucks," she said.

"Besides, I'm sure he must have gone on the tour bus. He stopped by his compartment right before the second bus left for the lake," I added, looking again toward the door. I badly wanted to get up and go see what he was doing, but forced myself to sit still.

"Do you want me to move?" Adam asked me.

"Huh?"

"You're positively humming with energy. I can feel how badly you want to flicker," he said softly so the waiter, who was serving people across the aisle from us, couldn't hear.

"Not flicker, just move." I took a deep breath, and made an effort to calm my jangly nerves. "I want to know where Alan Taylor went."

"And his wife?" Adam asked, giving me a highly disconcerting look. It just about pierced me down to my soul. "Or do you know where she is?"

"Not where she is, no," I answered.

He was silent for a moment, then put a hand on mine and gently squeezed my fingers. "Karma, if you know of a crime that's happened—"

"I don't know," I said, then shook my head. Pixie watched me closely. "No, that's not right. There was a crime. I've heard the proof of it."

"The domestic violence?" he asked.

"Yes."

"If you have evidence, then I can present it to the nearest Watch office. Which ... damn. We're almost to Bulgaria? That would be Sofia. After that, it's Istanbul."

"We don't go that close to Sofia," I said slowly. "And my evidence is kind of subjective. I don't know that it's enough to convict anyone. I feel like it would be better to get more."

"Like proof that Alan Taylor killed his wife?" Pixie asked, her voice low, but throbbing with excitement.

I cast her another glance, this time worried that her nervous energy would cause the glamour to crack, but she'd bought the industrial-strength kind, enough to withstand even an adolescent polter. "That would be nice, yes."

"What can I do to help you?" Adam asked, which earned him a smile, and a little stroke to his thigh.

"I appreciate you offering that without lecturing me, which I'm sure you're dying to do."

"Of course I am. But I know how serious this case is to you, and if I can help, I'm happy to do so."

"Honestly, I don't think there's much we can do without talking to Alan Taylor. But I suspect that is going to have to wait until after the party is over."

I was correct in that supposition. We finished dinner, and then returned to the lounge with the rest of the company, minus, I didn't hesitate to notice, Alan Taylor. There the murder-mystery event played out, with everyone submitting their guesses as to who did what, when, and to whom.

"Congratulations," I told Adam and Pixie, who had tied for first place with the English couple who had been sitting with Rev. Pixie clutched the bottle of what I assumed was very expensive champagne, as well as a teddy bear wearing the train steward's uniform. She almost danced with pleasure as she and Adam returned to where we'd been sitting for the explanation of the murder, and the awards. "I do hope you give that champagne to Adam. You can't have it once you're back home."

She made a face, but handed it over to him with only minor grousing. "All right, but I want credit for the fact that it was my lit deductions that got us the prize. All Adam did was ask people about what was their relationship to the missing bride. No one but me suspected that she was really her sister, Lady Waverly, in disguise. Are we going to stick it to Mr. Taylor now?"

I glanced at the clock. "It's too late for that. We'll talk to him in the morning. And by 'we,' I mean Adam and me."

"That's just mean," she said, but she was in too good of a mood to do more than complain for five minutes while we herded her back to our suite.

"Remember your promise," she told me twenty minutes later, casting a dark look at the closed door of the bathroom where Adam was getting ready for bed.

"We won't do anything but sleep." I patted her on her head as she curled up on the bed that Paolo had made out of the couch, and hurried into the bedroom before she could snap at me for such an action.

Adam entered a few minutes later, clad in a pair of plaid flannel pants and a T-shirt. "I gather we're not going to do anything that would require me to wear less clothing?" he asked as I pulled back the bedding on the other side of the bed.

"I promised Pixie, and to be honest …"

He nodded. "It would be a bit awkward, yes. She's just outside the door."

"Now, the hotel in Istanbul is another matter. That's a suite, too. Two bedrooms, two baths, little living room between them, according to the literature Lori gave me." I waggled my eyebrows at him. "Anything is fair game then."

"I will hold you to that," he said, climbing into bed, reaching for me. I snuggled into him, my body and brain buzzing with thoughts and emotions and sexual needs that I told myself would not be quenched that night. I felt jittery and slightly itchy, as if the air was filled with static.

"Do you want to talk about the case, or go to sleep?" he asked, trying hard to stifle a big yawn.

I was about to tell him that I'd welcome his thoughts, but realized then that with the long flight he must be exhausted.

"Sleep. We can talk tomorrow," I said, breathing deeply of his scent, relaxing against his warm, solid body.

Almost instantly, I felt his body sink into the mattress, his arms going boneless, his breathing deep and steady, with just the slightest hint of a snore.

I tried to force myself to sleep, but I couldn't seem to get comfortable, not even smooshed up against Adam.

I got up and paced the small space in the bedroom for about fifteen minutes, pulling open the curtains to watch the night scenery pass us by. Signs warned of a town coming up, Ruse, and almost immediately the train slowed down to a stop at the station. I rubbed my arms, wondering why I felt so wired. It was as if I were standing on a low-voltage electric fence, my body almost twitching with the need to move.

"Oh, for heaven's sake …" I whispered, and hurriedly yanked on the pair of black pants and the gray cashmere sweater that I'd worn earlier in the Budapest station. I was about to unload from my pockets the leftover money, receipts, and postcards from our shopping when Adam mumbled something in his sleep.

Not wanting to wake him with my fumbling around in the dark to find my bag, I eased the door open, half expecting Pixie to wake up when I slipped out of the bedroom, but she had her earbuds in, and was obviously sound asleep. I tiptoed my way out of the cabin, emerging into the corridor with a sigh of relief. Low lights dotted the wall, but to my surprise, Luc, the night attendant, wasn't in his chair.

I realized then that the train had pulled into the station, and feeling desperate for an outlet for my nerves, I decided to go to the lounge car. "It's only three," I said, squinting at the clock next to the attendant's chair. "The night owls will still be up in the bar car. Maybe a stiff drink will help knock me out."

Just as I passed the door to the next car, I glanced out the window, and staggered to a stop, staring with disbelief at the sight of Rennie walking along the platform, her head down, her hands thrust into the pockets of her brown dress.

"What the ever-loving hell?" I asked, and, without thinking, jerked open the door and hurried down the few steps onto the platform. It was chilly out, a breeze whipping along the platform that caused my hair to flutter in my face.

"Madame?" One of the attendants from another car stepped out and trotted over. "Did you need assistance?"

I pushed my hair off my face. "No thanks. Er … how long are we stopping here?"

He grimaced. "For about a quarter of an hour. There is a problem down the line, you understand. A tree fell, and it is being cleared. You wish to stroll, yes?"

I glanced back toward Rennie. "I thought if I would if we're stopped long enough."

"I will make sure to alert you before we set off again," he reassured me, then turned back when five men and four women spilled out of the bar car, still in murder-mystery costumes, and drunkenly called for the attendant to bring them more champagne. "You will excuse?" he said before hurrying off to no doubt warn them they didn't have too long to party on the platform.

I set off in the other direction toward Rennie, now standing under one of the yellow sodium station lights, staring out into the night.

Just as I was about to say her name, she turned and gave a little jump, one hand at her throat. "Oh, Karma! How you startled me. I wasn't expecting to see anyone at this time of night."

The partyers started singing in Italian.

"There's a few of us still awake," I said, studying her face. It told me little, since she bore the same worried expression I'd seen every other time. "Are you all right?"

"Not really, no. I thought I'd … I needed a bit of air. …" She seemed to crumple up on herself, tears welling up in her eyes. With a glance back at where the partyers were now dancing while one of them sang loudly and extremely off tune, I took her arm and escorted her over to a nearby bench. She collapsed down onto it, doubled over with her head in her hands.

I sat next to her, trying to figure out what was going on. It seemed like I had only just decided that Alan Taylor had killed his wife, and now here she was, apparently hale and hearty.

Apparently being the key, I decided.

She straightened up, her face blotchy with tears. "I'm so sorry. I've been nothing but bad news to you, haven't I? It's just that Alan … Alan's …" She gave a half sob, half hiccup. "Alan's disappeared."

"He *what?*" That was the last thing I expected her to say, and I was sure my expression showed my disbelief.

"I went to find him, and he's not in the compartment, and not in the lounge or any other public car. I'm worried, Karma. Very worried."

"Why?" I couldn't help but ask, then immediately felt guilty. "I'm sorry, that sounded callous and uncaring. If your husband is missing, then obviously, we must search for him in case he's injured and needs help. But … that aside, I'm confused. Are you worried because you think he might be hiding in an attempt to waylay you? If so, I should tell you that I have your phone, the one that your husband hid."

"You have it?" Her hand went back to her throat, fingers fluttering there for a few seconds. "You have my phone? The one with the recordings?"

"I do, and since you gave me permission, I listened to the audio." I gave her a long look. "What I heard there is definitely enough to bring to the attention of the police. Alan could be looking at serious jail time for his threats."

She shook her head, slumping back against the wall of the station. "It's not going to be that easy. Alan won't let attacks against him go unanswered. He will revenge himself upon anyone who did him wrong."

"If he's in jail, he can't harm you," I pointed out as gently as I could. Her emotions were so raw, I could almost feel the nervous energy originating in them.

"Perhaps, but it wasn't me I was speaking of." She gave me a look that made the hairs on my arms stand on end. "You and Pixie would be at risk. He would seek vengeance against you, and even if he was jailed, you'd still spend your lives looking over your shoulders. Alan is ruthless that way, and you'd be dead in his sights for what he believed was justice."

"I wasn't speaking of the mortal police when I mentioned jail," I said softly, an icy shiver down my spine making me twitchy. "The Otherworld Watch would take a hand in the situation."

"They can't," she argued. "He's mortal."

"One who married a vespillo, and is comfortable enough with us to visit a popular Otherworld bar in Paris." I gave her hand—as cold as the chill that kept making the skin on my back twitch—a squeeze, and added, "The Watch can take action against a mortal if he commits a felony against one of us." There was a wealth of meaning behind that last sentence.

Rennie's hand twitched beneath mine, her gaze sliding away. "That's so. But there is no proof. No solid proof. And without that, he'll destroy anyone who tries to bring him to justice. You don't understand how dangerous he is, Karma."

"Oh, I think I have a pretty good idea," I said slowly, my attention momentarily turned to three people who had left the drunken gang. Two women were doing what I could only think of as a TikTok dance down the platform toward us, followed by a man who called at them in a very proper English accent, "Don't go too far. Clarisse! Do you hear me? The train is stopped for only a few minutes."

Rennie made a faint noise of distress. "I can't—I don't want anyone to see me like this," she said quickly, wiping her eyes and leaping to her feet. "It's too much. It's all just too much."

She ran past the three people and entered the nearest carriage before I could do more than get to my feet.

"You are so straitlaced, Savian," one of the Italian women said when their companion rounded them up and herded them back to the main group, all of whom were now conducting a sporting event that consisted of attempts to jump over a freestanding bench. Several of them face-planted on the ground, but since all of them rose laughing wildly, I assumed no one was being hurt.

"Fine, we go, but you cannot join us again. You are no fun," the second TikTok woman said, and, grabbing her companion's hand, ran toward the others, calling something that in Italian that I didn't understand.

"Finally," I heard the man say as I slowly made my way past him toward the train. I was mulling over the conversation with Rennie, and wondering how I could initiate the train staff to conduct a search for the missing Alan, when the man called out to me, and approached with a pack of cigarettes in his hand. "Pardon, you don't happen to have a lighter or matches, do you?"

"Sorry," I said, pausing. He was tall and dark-haired, with one of those long faces that I equated with the English, and eyes that looked remarkably focused for someone who'd clearly spent the evening partying. He was dressed in a frock coat and top hat, and I had a vague memory of seeing him earlier in the evening, but I didn't remember him from the regular tourists. "I don't smoke, so I don't have either of those things."

He smiled. "That's all right. What I really want is you."

Before I could do more than gawk at him, he reached out and jabbed a needle into my neck. I felt myself falling even as my mouth was saying, "Hurn?"

TEN

Sound was the first thing that caught my attention from where I was floating on a midnight sea under an ebony sky.

"—it went fine, just fine, sweetheart. You worry too much, Maura, have I told you that lately?" The man's voice that spoke was vaguely familiar, rich with amusement and affection. "Yes, but you love that about me," he said after a moment's silence.

Maura? Who was this Englishman, and why was he in barging into my dreams?

Pain from a cramped leg caught my attention, and I attempted to shift in my sleep.

My cheek brushed an upholstered surface that in no way resembled the expensive bed linens used on the Byzantine Express.

"Love you, too. Kisses to Savvy. I should be home by this time tomorrow. I just have to turn over the subject in Bucharest, get my reimbursement—then I can portal my way back to you. I may have picked up a little something for you in Bucharest, before I got onto the train. No. No, just for you. Think garments. Skimpy garments."

A rich chuckle surrounded me as I clawed my way out of the black sea of oblivion. My eyes, after some fighting, opened, but they were blurry and out of focus. However, the flickering lights and feeling of motion beneath me warned I was not on the train.

"Well, yes, I guess you're right and it will be more for me than for you, although I promise if the thong part of said garment gets stuck in your butt, I shall be there to admire it. With both hands."

What the hell? I managed to raise my head, and squinted in order to bring the silhouetted head in front of me into more or less focus. It was a man. And if the pinpoints of light in front of us were anything to go by, we were in a car.

Not on the train, my brain pointed out the fact that had struck me a few seconds before. *You are no longer on the train.*

I was in a car, not on the train.

What the hell? my brain asked again as it fought to process facts. It felt like it was filled with molasses, thick and gloopy and unable to work with its usual speed and clarity.

Not on the train. I wasn't on the train. Pixie and Adam were on the train. So were Rennie and Alan Taylor, and everyone else, all speeding their way through the night to Istanbul.

I was not there with them. Panic hit me hard then, the sort of panic that has your heart pumping with fear, your mind focused on only one thing.

I was left behind. Everyone I loved in this part of the world was zipping off to Turkey, and I was here, in the car of someone I didn't know, having been drugged.

"Glarn," I heard someone said as I struggled to sit up, my arms and legs moving in a manner that seemed wholly disconnected with the rest of me. Blood pounded in my ears as I fought my way up.

"—and I'll kiss … hold up, Maura. I think the subject is awake." The seat beneath me moved, or at least that's what it felt like when I was thrown back before the car came to an abrupt stop. The silhouetted head in front of me turned to consider me. "Up, then, are you? I want no trouble, or I'll have to restrain you."

"Hrr?" I asked, before managing to bring a hand to my mouth, wondering what was wrong with it. "Who're you?"

"Talk to you later, my love. I must do the introduction and explanations. Yes, yes, I will. No, not even the slightest morsel of danger. You are my sun and moon and everything. Kiss the sprout for me again." The man touched a button on his steering wheel before saying, "The name is Savian Bartholomew, thief taker extraordinaire, if my wife is to be believed, and she never lies. You, I'm afraid to say, are now in my custody."

I said a very rude word.

"Quite," he said, before eyeing me carefully. "I should mention that I searched you for weapons, and have your phone up here, just in case you were tempted to call someone to aid you. How's your head feeling?"

"Like it's full of thick, viscous substances," I said slowly, trying to process what he was saying. The words had meaning that I knew, but I couldn't seem to catch more than a glimpse of them before they flitted out of my awareness. My heart rate started to slow, but I still felt jittery with panic.

"I'm afraid that's a side effect of the drug. The good news is that it should pass fairly quickly now that you're awake and moving about. Although, please, not too much movement. I would like to get us to Bucharest in one piece." He turned around and pulled out onto the road again.

Without thinking, I reached for the car door. I didn't have a plan, just felt it was necessary to know if I had options.

The door refused to open.

"Child locks are so useful, don't you find?" he said in his upper-crust English voice, now full of amusement.

"You took me off the train," I said, thoughts slowly starting to coalesce in my sluggish brain.

"On the contrary—I took you from the platform upon which you were taking a constitutional."

"The train has left by now, surely. They were only stopped for fifteen minutes."

"This is so. I'm glad to see the old thought process-es are starting to chug along," he said in an agreeable tone.

Suddenly, I wanted to punch the back of his head. How dare he be so pleasant when he was kidnapping me?

"This is kidnapping," I pointed out.

"It isn't, you know. I realize it may seem like it to you, but I am a thief taker, a member of the L'au-dela, and hired to find and transport individuals wanted for various reasons. A complaint has been lodged against you and I was sent to remove you from a problematic situation. I'll show you my credentials when we stop. It shouldn't be much longer. We're coming into Bucharest now."

I looked over his shoulder, squinting at the bright lights of an oncoming car, noticing the tall span that warned we were coming up to a bridge. "Give me back my phone. I want to call my … well, boyfriend, I guess. He's with the Watch."

"Mm-hmm. I would, but you see, I have a rule against that sort of thing. It just leads to trouble until we get to our destination. Once we're there, I will hand you over to the Committee. No doubt they will allow you to make a call."

The Committee. Damn, they were the umbrella for organizations like the Akashic League, and had some say in what its members did. Obviously, someone at the League had asked them to pick me up.

"I want my phone," I repeated, anger triggering another burst of adrenaline, which did much to push out the mind molasses.

"Sorry, no can do."

"You drugged me. You shot something straight into my neck."

"I did. It's an extremely effective drug that ensures I can take subjects with a minimum of risk to everyone involved. It's the safest way to take people into custody, I assure you."

"You are a bad man," I told him, frustrated and suddenly filled with nervous energy. "Only bad men drug other people and kidnap them."

"I'm not bad, although I suppose I can see why you might think that. Later, hopefully, you will see the charm that my wife says fairly oozes out of me."

"Not only that," I said, feeling particularly aggrieved, frustrated at the lack of my ability to reason with him, and annoyed that the League would do this when I had promised I'd turn myself in to their office in Istanbul. You'd think that after I worked for them my whole life, they could cut me a little slack, but no. "You work for people who are equally bad."

"On the contrary, my friend is one of the nicest people I know."

"Friend?" I asked, confused, noting that Savian was slowing down as he approached the bridge.

"A friend of mine lodged the harassment complaint against you. Well, that was the technical cause, but the truth is, he doesn't want to see people getting hurt. He asked me to do him a favor, and since I've known him forever, I couldn't resis—"

I went full polter on him just as he was approaching the bridge. I flung myself forward, flickering back and forth across the front seat, his scream of surprise echoing loudly in my ears even as the car jerked off the road and onto the verge, heading for a dense clump of shrubs that clung to the edge of a cliff face. I didn't have time to brace myself before the car slammed into the shrubs and cliff, sending me to the floor of the front seat.

An explosion above me filled the air with dust and sound that I fought to escape, and even though my polter blood was diluted by a mortal mother, I found myself standing outside the car, panting and shaking with the effects of the crash, not sure how I got there.

Savian was slumped to the side, the airbag holding him pinned at an odd angle against the back seat.

"Oh, goddess," I said, hurrying back to the car, climbing in the passenger side to check him over.

He moaned, but was out, a thin trickle of blood seeping from a cut on his eyebrow. His pulse seemed to be strong enough, however, and a quick examination didn't reveal any other injuries.

"I don't think you're seriously injured, but I'll call for an ambulance nonetheless," I told him, fishing my phone out from where it had fallen into the footwell. "Not that you deserve it after shooting me up with who-knows-what, but still. I don't want you hurt because you were idiotic enough to listen to a friend."

I clambered out of the car, poking at my phone, but it refused to respond. The screen was cracked, and I had a horrible fear that it had been broken in the crash. A quick search of the front seat yielded Savian's phone … in three pieces. Damn.

I spun around, looking for a business or house where I could seek help, but we were in the outskirts of town, which appeared to be confined solely to industrial small businesses. "And they're all closed," I said on a sigh. "Because anything else would be too convenient."

It took me a half hour's hike into Bucharest before I got to a gas station that was open, and begged the use of a phone from the man at the counter. I called for medical aid for the thief taker, then turned my attention back to the man hovering next to me. "I need to catch up to the Byzantine Express. Do you know it?"

He frowned, his English much better than my attempt at French and German. "Is not here."

"Right. It's on its way to Istanbul. I got … er … hell, I don't know how to explain what happened. I was at the station where it was stopped; then it left. Without me."

It took another five minutes of a variety of languages and an online translation website before I made my problem clear to him. At that point, he pursed his lips. "It is a man you left on the train?"

He was an older man, reminding me a lot of my maternal grandfather, with lots of crow's-feet, balding gray hair, and a habit of squinting that warned his vision wasn't great.

I debated denying that it was because Adam was on the train, but then realized that the thought of sweethearts being separated was probably going to be a point in my favor, so I adopted a lovelorn expression. "Yes, a very dear man. One I … well, I don't know what our future will bring, but I know I want him in it."

He nodded. "Is good. You should be with man." He consulted his phone again, then tapped a few times before pulling up a website in Romanian. Ten minutes later, my new friend Gregor and I determined that the train was going to be in the town of Varna at six in the morning, and if I hurried, I might be able to get a flight out there in time.

"You're sure about the airplane?" I asked, emerging from the gas station office when Gregor's son-in-law pulled alongside us in a beat-up black truck that clearly was used on a farm.

Gregor gave instructions to his son-in-law in rapid Romanian before turning back to me to say in French, "Yes, plane to Varna. Many businessmen, you know?"

"Commuter flight, eh? That'll do," I said, and tried to press a little of the money in my pocket on him, but he refused.

"Is good you be with man," he said, then grasped me firmly by the shoulders and kissed both of my cheeks before boosting me up into the truck.

The next hour and a half was mostly a blur of lights, faces, and languages I didn't understand, but at last I found myself emerging from a small plane that evidently hopped from Hungary to Romania and Turkey every morning. I had sent up a mental thanks that I still had my passport from the visit to the train-station currency exchange, or I would never have been able to catch up to the train.

The flight, the taxi to the train station, and my tip to Gregor's son-in-law ate up the remainder of my shopping money, so I prayed that nothing else would go awry.

"This is ridiculous," I told myself as I paced up and down the platform waiting for my train, glancing at the clock every minute or so. "It hasn't come yet. The train isn't going to suddenly change their route. The man in the station said it would be here. It's going to be here. Stop being so panicky."

I continued to pace, glance at the clock, and wish like hell my phone worked so I could check in with Pixie and Adam.

By the time the familiar blue-and-cream-colored train cars rolled to a stop on the platform, I was almost dancing with the need to get on board.

One of the attendants opened the door to a car and trotted down the steps at the same time a bunch of trolleys, filled with fresh food for the restaurant cars, rolled up to the end of the train.

"Madame?" the attendant asked, blinking in surprise at me.

"Hi. Yes, it's me. Got ... er ... it's a long story. I really need to go check on my ward and friend." I was up the stairs and racing through the cars before he could respond.

Although most of the compartments were left unlocked during the day, since attendants in the cars were ever present, at night people locked them, and given that it was only a little after six in the morning, I was fumbling with my key when the door was suddenly flung open, causing me to squeak and leap backward.

Adam stood in the doorway, an Adam with blazing pale blue eyes, his hair almost standing on end, and an expression of what very much looked like fury. "Karma!" he said in a volume that could be called a roar.

"Adam!" I said, so happy to see him that I flung myself onto him, wrapping my arms around him.

Over his shoulder, Pixie rose from where she'd been curled up with a blanket on a chair, her expression wary.

"Deus, what happened to you?" she said, her expression turning to one of intense curiosity. "You look terrible."

"Are you all right?" Adam said, prying me off his chest in order to give me a quick examination.

Aware of Paolo and two other attendants approaching down the corridor at a fast clip, I answered, "Yes, not hurt, although I'm sure I look as bad as the face Pixie is making. One sec. Yes, it's me, and everything is fine. There was a misunderstanding with a … friend … in Ruse who decided to show me … his house, and I missed getting back to the station in time. No, no, no harm done. I'm here safe and sound, as you can see. I'm so sorry if there's been any trouble."

Paolo spent several minutes telling me how relieved he was that I had made it back, curiosity evident on his face, as well, but he was either too polite or too mindful of company policy regarding clients' privacy to press me for details.

"Dear goddess, I never want to go through the last few hours again," I said, closing the door at last, turning to face Adam and Pixie.

"A friend picked you up to show you his house?" Pixie said, shooting Adam a thoughtful look. "Wow. Just … wow."

Adam stood with his arms crossed, looking particularly immovable and, at that moment, more than a little suspicious. "What really happened?"

I plucked one of the bottles of mineral water from our stash and plopped down in a chair, not even bothering with a glass. I swigged half the bottle of water before answering. "So much that I don't even know if

I can sort it all out. But I'll start. Wait—it's only six in the morning. Paolo said you had been searching the train for the last hour. Why?"

"Why did I search for you when I woke up and found you missing?" The look Adam shot me spoke volumes, and none of them reported with any kindness on my mental fortitude.

"Aww." I patted his hand when he sat down opposite me, Pixie reclaiming her bed, still swathed in blankets. "Thank you for caring."

"If you weren't, at this moment, looking like you have been dragged backward through a series of hedges, I would take umbrage at the implication that I would allow anyone to disappear without a trace, let alone a woman who badly wants into my pants."

The resulting "Ew" that emerged from Pixie was muffled by a prodigious yawn.

"We can continue this in the bedroom," I told Adam, nodding toward Pixie. "She probably wants to go back to sleep."

"Deus! I deserve to hear what happened to you as much as he does," she said, sitting up straight, her hair—now that the glamour was off—a mass of black that resembled a stork's nest on top of her head. An untidy stork's nest.

"All right, but I do want to make it fast. For one, I want a shower. And for another, I'm exhausted. Drugs, adrenaline, the car crash … it all takes its toll, you know?"

Both of them stared at me in matching pointed fashions.

"Right," I said, and, taking another swig off the water bottle, started my tale. "I couldn't sleep, so I thought I'd work off a bit of the polter energy in the club car with all the people still partying. On my way there, I saw Rennie on the platform. We were stopped at Ruse at that point."

"Rennie?" Adam frowned. "Are you sure it was her?"

"Yup." I recounted the conversation I had with her.

Adam's gaze was on the water bottle that sat between us, his brows fully pulled together in what I was coming to recognize as his thinking face. "You are certain that she said her husband was missing?"

"I don't normally mistake conversations," I said, faintly offended that he would call my statement into question.

He shook his head, his gaze now searching mine. "I didn't mean to question what you heard—but you clearly have suffered from some trauma. You mentioned being drugged and in a car crash. I assume that means you were kidnapped, and all of those events can lead to confused memories."

"I'm sure they can," I said, mollified. Once a cop, always a cop, I said to myself with a little smile. "But in this case, I'm quite sure of what she said. Why do you ask, other than the obvious? You haven't seen Alan, have you?"

"Yes," he said, taking me by surprise.

"What?" I sat up straight, feeling my jaw sagging a little. I snapped my mouth shut before asking, "When?"

"When we were searching the train for you. I made the stewards check all the compartments." He rubbed his jaw, and one side of his mouth quirked up. "There are a whole lot of people who wouldn't mind seeing me pushed off the train because of that, but I couldn't risk someone hiding you somewhere."

"Under the seat like in one of the Agatha Christies," Pixie said, her bird's nest nodding from the depths of her blankets.

I pushed aside the memory of my time in Alan's compartment hiding under the seat. "But that doesn't make sense. Rennie was adamant that he was missing. She was so distressed."

"We'll talk to them both later," Adam said, rubbing his chin again, grimacing briefly at the sound of his bristles on his fingers.

It sent a sensual shiver down my spine, but knowing that Pixie would not appreciate me telling him that, I continued my narration with the kidnapping by Savian the thief taker.

"I knew it," Adam said when I finished.

"Don't you even think about looking martyred," I told him, pointing a finger at his face, which did, in fact, sport a distinct martyred appearance. "I'm the one that got shot in the neck with drugs, hauled off to a car, and was about to be turned over to the Bucharest Committee on a complaint that is complete and utter bullshit."

"What complaint?" Pixie asked, yawning again. "The one from the League?"

To my surprise, Adam was silent for almost a minute. Then he gave a sharp nod. "I agree with your conclusion."

"What conclusion?" Pixie pushed down the front of her blanket cocoon to glare at us. "What do you guys know that you're not saying?"

"It's the only thing I can think of that makes sense," I told Adam, my fingers tracing the pattern of wood on the table.

"What makes sense? Deus! Why are you keeping things from me? It's to make me feel stupid, isn't it? I'm going to tell Dr. Wellbottom that you're deliberately trying to undermine my mental stability!"

I shot her a look that said I didn't appreciate her comment, and answered, "We're not keeping anything from you, Pixie, nor are we trying to make you feel stupid. Also, we will talk later about the use of threats to report me as a bargaining chip, and why they won't ever work."

She sank back into her blankets and muttered something that I thought it best not to hear.

"Karma has drawn the conclusion, and I agree with her, that the person who arranged for the warrant against her was Alan Taylor," Adam told Pixie in a tone that dripped with both patience and a long-suffering resignation that came from having lived through his own daughter's teenage years.

"Alan?" she asked, surprised enough to set aside her sulking. "Why would he—oh, to get her in trouble?"

I exchanged glances with Adam, who gave a little nod. "More, I think, to get me out of the way."

"Because you were helping Rennie? That's heinous! He had to know you would, like, tell the Watch people what he was doing?"

"I'm sure he knew that was possible, but you see, he knew something that until very recently I did not."

She looked first at me, then to Adam, then back to me, finally wrestling the blankets off her so that she could slap down all four hands. "GAH! You guys are so annoying! I could just scream!"

"Please don't. I don't need Paolo concerned about what's going on. Before you blow a gasket—"

"I don't have gaskets!" she said with outrage, but immediately picked up her phone, no doubt to look up what a gasket was.

"—I will tell you what should have been obvious." I stopped, and frowned for a few seconds. "No, that's not fair. It wasn't obvious."

"That's telling on its own," Adam said, one finger rubbing his lower lip.

I refused to allow myself to be distracted, even though I badly wanted to get him into the bedroom so I could kiss the hell out of that lip.

"That's it," Pixie declared, standing up, her wad of blankets slithering down her body to pool around her feet. "I'm leaving. You guys are too deranged to live with."

"Sit down. The obvious thing that wasn't at all obvious even though it should be is that Rennie isn't being abused by her husband for the simple reason that she's not alive. She's a spirit."

Pixie gawked at me for a full ten seconds before she bent, scooped up her blankets, and got back onto her bed. "Tell me everything you know," she said in her best detective voice.

"All right." I ignored the pointed look Adam gave me. "Do you remember our talk at home about necromancers and vespillos?"

She nodded.

"In short, there are four types of spirits. Most of them happily reside in the spirit world, and don't touch ours."

"OK," Pixie said, and reached for her notebook.

"The second type are the ones bound to a location. They can be drawn forth by a Summoner, appear on their own accord if they have ample energy to do so, or can be resurrected by a necromancer, via a vespillo."

"That's what Rennie was," Pixie said, nodding, and making notes.

"That's right. Those spirits come in many flavors, and can interact with the mortal world, or not, again depending on their ability to manifest energy. There are also special cases, some spirits that are corporeal due to extraordinary circumstances, like interference by necromancers, demon lords, or others who have power over spirits."

"Is that what Olga and Teo are?" she asked.

"Yes. They are grounded, and can appear in the mortal world when they summon enough energy. Just like Adam's spirits."

Adam nodded. "A Summoner brought forth Jules and Anthony for me, and grounded them. They can leave if they wanted, but they choose to stay."

"The third type of spirit is called an Alastor."

"You mentioned them before. So, they're what? Special?" she asked, still taking notes.

"Very much so. Usually, they have ties with a demon lord, but it's not always the case. They have a strong link to the mortal world, and can more or less interact at will."

"Alastor," Pixie repeated. "Demon lord. Ick. What about the fourth type?"

I hesitated, then shook my head. "I think we'll save discussion about them for another time. They aren't important or pertinent here."

She looked suspicious, but let it go. "So, you're saying Rennie is one of those three types? Which one? And how do you know?"

"I know because I have more than twenty years' experience as a TAE," I answered. "Although I admit that I've never seen an Alastor before. They're fairly rare and, when they want to, can appear mortal. Which is why I was taken in by Rennie looking like she was still living."

"Why didn't she tell you what she was?" Pixie asked.

"That's a very good question." I glanced at Adam but found no answers there. "I don't know. Fear, maybe?

She might have believed I wouldn't help her because she was a spirit; if that was the case, then maybe she thought to manipulate me into doing so by appearing alive."

"From what you've said, it would seem she's afraid of her husband," Adam said slowly. "But that doesn't explain why she wouldn't have sought aid from the Watch. She has to know we would have dealt with her abusive husband or, at the very least, protected her from further abuse."

"People who are in the middle of an abusive relationship don't always see options that the rest of us do," I said, thinking back on a domestic-abuse awareness class I'd taken a decade before. "Perhaps it's as simple as her not believing that anyone will help her. That fits with why her friend asked me to come here—oh goddess, Lori. I'll have to tell her that Rennie is an Alastor."

Adam looked at me as another thought dawned, one so profound, I had to think about it for half a minute. "Unless she knows," I said slowly.

"Who, Lori?" Pixie asked. "Why would she know that?"

"Because she used to be a necromancer," Adam said, his gaze serious on mine.

"Do me a favor," I said, staring at him, my mind whirling. "Would you use your magical marshal and Watch power to look up Alan Taylor and see what you find about him?"

"Oooh," Pixie said, scrunching down farther in her blanket nest. "Things are getting deep!"

"He's American, mortal … ah. He is sole owner of a chain of theaters catering to Otherworld entertainment." Adam looked up. "The kind that put on live shows. He's got a dozen of them across the US."

"Dad took me to one of those a few years ago," I said, trying to make puzzle pieces fit together in my mind. "It was packed."

"According to this …" Adam whistled, his eyebrows raised. "He's definitely in the seven-figure wealth range."

Pixie set down her notebook. "What does that mean for us?"

"It means that we're hearing two conflicting stories from two different sets of people, and I don't know which one to believe. Or why one of them would lie." I rubbed my forehead as if that would help me think better.

"So what are we going to do now?" Pixie asked.

I shifted the rubbing to my temples. "I can tell you what I'm not going to do—I'm not going to turn myself in to Istanbul without having resolved the situation with Rennie and Alan Taylor. Time to make a battle plan."

ELEVEN

"I am definitely not going to win the Most Popular award on this trip," Adam groused when he met us outside our compartment. "Especially if I wake up people a second time."

"It's after eight," I pointed out. "The first breakfast will start soon, so folks should be up and about. I take it you didn't find Alan?"

"No. And the steward in Alan's car is not very happy with me demanding to open his compartment because I was 'worried about his well-being,'" Adam answered, putting air quotes around the last four words.

"That can't be helped. So Alan really is missing. Hmm."

"He wasn't in the public cars or his compartment, so I think we can take that as given." Adam glanced at his phone when it pinged at him.

"That just means we're going to have to do this the hard way. Is everyone clear as to what they're doing?"

"There's only three of us, Karma," Pixie pointed out, her glamour firmly in place. She had once again chosen not to wear her lady archaeologist outfit, and was instead clad in her peacock lounging pajamas. "It's not like there's that much going on. You and I are searching the back cars, and Adam is doing the front ones."

"Yes, but it's polite when setting out with a grand plan to make sure that everyone knows exactly what they're doing," I said, my gaze meeting Adam's.

He had been looking at his phone. "My boss got the text I sent earlier."

My stomach felt like it dropped down to my feet. "Oh?"

"He had a few choice things to say about what's going on."

My shoulders slumped. Dammit, I knew I should have begged Adam not to report in to his boss, but I couldn't do that. He loved his job, and it wasn't fair of me to ask him to go against dearly held principles. "I'm sure he did. So that's it, then."

"Not quite." To my surprise, Adam smiled. "He didn't outright order me to take you into custody, but he said that if I didn't do so, I would have to answer to the local Watch office for my inaction regarding the situation."

"Why are you smiling if you're going to get in trouble for not taking me into custody?" I asked, confused.

"Who says I'm not?" He didn't even glance at Pixie before pulling me into an embrace and saying against my lips, "Consider yourself my prisoner," just before he kissed me.

We both ignored Pixie's assorted gagging sounds, but managed to part without me rubbing myself all over him as I badly wanted.

"Oh, please," I told Pixie when Adam turned and marched off to start at the front of the train, and work back in an attempt to locate Alan Taylor. "It was just a kiss. You should be able to cope with the sight of us kissing. You keep telling me you aren't a child."

A mutinous expression flitted across her face. "Now you're using my own words against me. Low blow, Karma! Low blow."

"Yes, it is, and I'll apologize later, when I have time," I said, blithely ignoring her sputters of protest as we headed to the last couple of cars on the train. Paolo had referred to them as support cars, with sleeping quarters for staff, storage of passenger extra luggage, supplies, etc.

Luck, for once, was working for us in that almost all the staff were busy in other areas of the train, bringing people breakfast, tidying up compartments, waiting on the people who went to eat in the restaurant car, or even in the lounge. We managed to slip into the back two cars without having to explain to anyone what we were doing there. The end car consisted of luggage and stores, arranged with tidy precision.

"Who knew there were so many towels?" Pixie said, peering into one of the bins. "There must be a couple hundred here."

"Rich people demand fresh towels every day," I said, moving along the stacks of luggage, peering around and behind them. No one was hiding in the car.

"What I want to find is their chocolate stash."

"Their what?" I asked, finding my large suitcase that Pixie and I had used to hold our "tourist in Istanbul" clothing. I checked it, but it didn't appear to be tampered with, not that I had any expectation that it would.

"Those little chocolates that they put on our bed at night? I think I'm addicted to them. I asked Paolo if I could have two, and he said he'd try, but that they had a limited amount."

"Oh, those. You can have mine. I don't like dark chocolate."

She brightened up at the thought, and made no complaints when we had to hide behind a stack of suitcases as one of the stewards rushed into the room, gathered up an armful of towels, and hustled off.

"Next up, service car," I said, glancing down the corridor before bending over the lock.

"You're going to teach me how to do that, right?" Pixie asked as I manipulated the set of lockpicks that Adam had given me earlier. Evidently, he'd used them to great effect while he searched the train for me, and let me borrow them only when I swore I wouldn't use them on any compartments where passengers resided.

"You'd do better to ask my father, since he's the one who taught me how to pick locks. Ah. There it goes. You stand guard and warn me if anyone comes."

"Fine, but if you run across Alan Taylor's dead body, you have to let me see before you call Adam."

I gave her a long, long look. "We're going to talk to Dr. Wellbottom about getting you in for a second weekly session when we get back home."

"Oh, puh-lease," she said with accompanying eye roll. "Like she doesn't already want me to come in every day?"

"Just warn me if someone appears," I told her, and slipped into the darkened room.

The windows were covered, leaving the storage area dark and close feeling, the air somewhat stuffy. As I paused to get my bearings, wondering if I dared turn on a light, I heard something.

The slight rustling sent immediate goose bumps down my arms, and a jab of fear that had me pressing back against the door.

I wasn't alone.

Here's the thing about polters—we take to shadows like … well, like we're part of the shadows themselves. Put a polter in a darkened room, and if she doesn't want you to see her, you won't. I slid along the wall, silent as a wraith, my eyes searching the dimly lit room, aware of everything from the slightest creaking of the car as the train left the station, to a faint draft coming from an improperly sealed window.

And then I heard the rustle again. For a moment, I wondered if it was a rodent, but it was followed by a second noise, this one sounding like someone whose shoe had bumped into a piece of furniture, followed by an almost silent intake of breath.

Almost silent.

I reached out and flipped on the light, moving faster than I had in a very long time toward the source of the noise. A faint shriek followed as Rennie jumped at least six inches straight up.

"What on earth are you doing hiding in here?" I asked, my heart beating wildly as I tried to control my desire to shake her.

"It's Alan," she gasped, her arms wrapped around herself. "He's in a rage. I had to hide."

"Wait, what? You told me he was missing, that he'd disappeared." I studied her face, but it told me nothing. She wore the same expression of distress that I'd seen other times.

"He was. At least, I thought he was." She unwrapped her arms to make a vague gesture toward the door. "But then I saw him, and he was insane with anger."

"About what?" I asked, feeling itchy again, as if a thousand little ants were crawling over my flesh.

"You." She put a hand toward my arm, but snatched it back before actually touching me. "He knows everything, Karma. Knows that you were sent here to help me escape him, knows that you stole my phone from his bag, knows that you won't stop until you see justice for his crimes."

I blinked at that last bit, but my mind, ever one to follow its own path and not do what was expected, latched on to a lesser point. "How does he know I took the phone?"

"What?" She looked momentarily discombobulated, her hands moving in more vague gestures. "How does he know?"

"Yes." I was silent a moment, then asked, "Did you tell him?"

"No! Oh no! He knows because he had the camera in a small bag with his toiletries, and he said that later, the bag was moved from where he'd placed it."

I stared at her, the memory of being hidden under the seat in Alan's compartment still fresh in my mind. "That's unfortunate," I said slowly, getting the answer I needed about which of them was lying.

Alan had taken the toiletries bag with him before I found the phone.

"Very unfortunate. Oh, Karma, I can't tell you how much danger you are in, both you and your ward. He'll kill you if you don't get away now, while you still can. He's beyond reason."

"Why would—"

"He's deranged!" she interrupted in a near shriek, then, before I could say anything more, flung herself past me and had the door open and was out it.

"Hey," I heard Pixie say as she ran past her, disappearing into the next car. "Karma?"

"Right here," I said, standing in the open doorway.

"What's going on?" Pixie asked.

I gave her a brief rundown of what Rennie had said, ending with, "You're going to find Adam, that's what's going on."

"Are you kidding? I'm not going to leave you alone. What if Alan Taylor finds you?"

"I highly doubt he would do anything even if he did," I told her, making shooing motions. "Go find Adam and tell him to come here. I want to look over the compartment. I have a feeling there was a reason Rennie was in there other than trying to hide from her husband."

"I'll text him," she said, patting a pocket, then made a face. "Dammit! I left my phone in our compartment. I'll be right back. Don't do anything fun until I get back." She ran off, her short bob ruffling as a result.

I returned to the compartment, closing the door lest any of the staff return, and stood considering it. It appeared to be a stripped-down sleeping compartment, with the upper bunk and table having been removed. A smooth curved wooden panel on the left made up what I assumed was the lower seat pushed up, getting it out of the way for cleaning and such. With the light on, I could see that the window wasn't just blocked by curtains—several cases of champagne, wine, and various other alcohol were pushed up against it. To the right, more cases of champagne sat alongside several smaller cardboard boxes stamped with the logo of the train.

"And just what were you doing hiding behind these boxes, Rennie?" I murmured to myself as I moved over to open the nearest one.

It was filled with stationery provided to each compartment. The next two contained an assortment of items varying from spare light bulbs to bottles of upholstery cleaner. "And I will not be telling Pixie about this," I said, firmly putting the lid down on a deep box that bore tiny packages of chocolates.

A click sounded behind me, causing me to whirl around.

Alan Taylor stood at the door, twisting the lock, his eyes narrowed on me as he did so.

"What do you think you're doing?" I asked, incredulous.

"Taking care of a problem I should have dealt with days ago. You just can't stop snooping, can you?" he said, moving toward me with a near swagger. He stopped about a yard away, swaying slightly when the train swung around a bend.

"I was asked to check on Rennie by a friend who was worried about her," I said, moving slowly to put the boxes between us. I wasn't expecting an attack, but it never hurt to be cautious. "That can hardly be considered to be snooping."

"Searching my things can be, though, as can stealing my property. I want the phone you stole from me. And don't deny that you took it, because I know you did."

Another piece of the puzzle slid together. I gazed at Alan, trying to find visual proof of what I suspected, but finding none.

Alastors, I remembered, could be very convincing when they wanted.

"Not even going to deny it?" he asked, his voice harsh.

"Yes, of course I took the phone," I said calmly, far more calmly than I felt. I hoped Pixie wouldn't try to get into this compartment after she texted Adam. The last thing I needed was to have her in a dangerous situation. "Just as I was intended to do. As I was intended to listen to the recordings. Recordings, I might add, that were oddly open to differing interpretations."

"I don't know what you're talking about. But I do know you stole something from me," he almost crowed. "That makes this all so much more satisfying. Give me back the phone, Karma Marx."

"Naw, I think I'll hand it over to the Watch, instead. There's some pretty juicy evidence on there."

"The Watch," he said, scoffing, and took a step forward. "They won't do a damn thing to me. I'm mortal."

"Yes, Alan Taylor is mortal … but Rennie isn't."

He hesitated, eyes narrowing before he asked, "What the hell is that supposed to mean?"

"Just what I said. Alan is mortal, but Alastors aren't. There's nothing to stop me from banishing one to the Akasha."

Alan froze for a few seconds, but suddenly relaxed and gave a half smile. "You can't do that. You've been forbidden to use your extermination powers without being tossed in the Akasha, yourself."

"Odd how you know that fact," I said, shifting slightly to the side, trying to put a little more space between us. "I can't see any reason that Alan Taylor would be in possession of that knowledge. His wife, however … now, I can see Rennie knowing that, especially considering her friend Lori is the one who sent me off to look for her. In fact, I—"

I didn't see it coming. I'm both surprised and disappointed that my half-polter blood didn't warn me of an attack a fraction of a second before he struck me, but it didn't, and before I could blink, I was first slammed against the wall behind me, then flung across the compartment like I was a rag doll. I crashed painfully into the tucked-up lower seat, my head cracking against a stationary armrest, causing me to momentarily black out.

When I regained my senses, I was lying on my back on the floor, staring up as Alan Taylor hefted a bottle of champagne, raising it over his head, obviously about to slam it down onto my head.

I lunged forward, wrapping myself around his legs in an attempt both to protect my brains from being bashed in by expensive champagne and to make him fall over. A crashing noise from my right mingled with his scream of anger when I tried to pull his feet out from under him.

Pain exploded on my back just as another crash sounded, followed by a rush of wind, and then Adam's deep voice was there rumbling around the room as he demanded to know what was going on.

I lay collapsed on the floor, tears flowing at the sharp pain on the right side of my back, trying to move out of the way when Alan Taylor made a dash out of the room, but luckily, Adam had too much experience with both mortals and immortals to allow anyone to escape him. He jerked Alan back, spun him around, and, with both arms twisted behind him, snarled the Otherworld version of Miranda rights.

"Are you OK?" Pixie asked, hurrying to my side, her face tight with fear. She tried to help me up but, as the train swayed around another turn, fell backward onto the upraised seat, which gave a muffled click and then tumbled down into its normal position.

The body of a man rolled off the seat and hit the floor next to where I was now kneeling.

We all looked at it.

Adam sighed from where he stood over a feebly struggling Alan Taylor, having finished his warning.

"Did you do that?" he asked me, nodding at the body that nestled up against my leg.

I shot him a glare that, by rights, should have stripped all his lovely curls right off his thick head.

"That's …" Pixie blinked at the body, then looked over at Alan. "That's Alan Taylor. He's dead. But that's him, too. Is he a spirit?"

"Yes, but that's not Alan," I said, wincing and stifling a yelp when, with Pixie's help, I managed to get to my feet. "Rennie is an Alastor."

"Rennie Taylor, I place upon you this Bête Noire, which will not be removed until such time as the L'au-dela Watch deems it appropriate. You are under arrest," Adam said, pulling out not only a pair of zip ties but a small piece of parchment bearing a spell that he promptly cast.

"That's Rennie?" Pixie asked, staring with open-mouthed wonder at what appeared to be Alan Taylor.

"Yes. Ow. So much ow."

"But …" Pixie's face swam in front of me. Black splotches started to appear, making me blink furiously to clear my vision.

"She's wearing a glamour," I said, then added as the pain got to be too much for me, "I think … oh goddess … I think I'm going to …"

The faint swallowed me up, allowing me to drift off on a cloud of insensibility.

TWELVE

"Are you sure you're up to this?"

I was about to take a deep breath, remembered that such things were not allowed until my two cracked ribs healed up, and instead nodded. "I'd much rather curl up in the hotel bed and sleep a week or so, but I promised the League I'd do this, so I'm going to. Also, I imagine you'd get in hot water if I didn't."

"Not particularly. While you were seeing the doctor and getting patched up, I turned in my report," Adam answered. "Do you need more pain medicine, speaking of that? You look pale."

I hesitated, then pulled out a small prescription bottle from my bag. "I don't want to take a full dose, since that knocks me out, but maybe half of that will let me get through the proceedings without screaming in pain."

He waited until I took the pill before escorting Pixie and me toward a beautiful old building in Istanbul. It was a warm afternoon, the air filled with not only the soft buzzing of drowsy bees but liquid birdsong. The trees surrounding the building that housed the Watch's offices rustled in a manner that made me think of lazy summer afternoons of my childhood spent lying under a rhododendron bush with a stack of books.

"Maybe it's the drugs, but can we stay here after I explain everything?" I asked, nodding toward a stretch of white stone patio that was dotted with comfortable lounges, just perfect for sunning oneself.

"The sun is evil," Pixie said, hoisting her paper parasol higher. She had decided to continue her 1920s theme, and was wearing a genuine vintage flapper dress, this one striped blue and white, with a matching parasol.

"Not if you take precautions, but that's not what Karma asked, and the answer is we probably won't have time. I expect first seeing the Watch, then your session with the League is going to take some time," Adam answered.

The building we approached resembled an Ottoman-influenced Mediterranean villa, with white stone walls, red tiled roof, and beautiful scrollwork decorations along with metal filigree touches along the arched windows and doors.

"Remind me to get some selfies of us at this door," I told Pixie as we entered what I could describe only as a grand entrance, complete with massive stone roof over a protruding entranceway, blue-gray polished marble columns, arched doorway topped with an escutcheon set over stained glass atop a brass-studded door. It was an entrance intended on making an impression, and it did its job.

"Yeah, it's pretty all that, huh?" she answered, her eyes wide as we stepped into an equally grand entrance hall. Fortunately for those of us who were prone to gawking at the scenery, two men came forward immediately, one stopping to speak with Adam, while the second stopped in front of Pixie and me.

"Ms. Marx? I'm Durrell, Alasdair Durrell. I'm the director of the Akashic League."

"Deus," Pixie said under her breath.

I knew just how she felt. I shook the hand Alasdair offered, feeling like my insides had turned to cement. "I would say it's a pleasure to meet you, but I gather you being called to Istanbul means that the League considers my situation nothing short of dire."

He gave a little laugh, surprising me, since he didn't have the air of doom and gloom that I felt wrapped around me. "It's certainly not a situation I'd suggest undergoing simply for the experience, but I don't think it's quite at the dire state." His gaze shifted over to where Adam and the second man were in quiet discussion. "At least, not so far as the League is concerned. The Watch might have other issues to … discuss."

I sighed heavily, wanting to slump, but that would hurt my ribs, so instead, I followed Alasdair through the gorgeous gray marble and stone hall to one of the side rooms. This was also done in stone, with beautiful tapestries on one wall, columns marching down another, and a third that faced a garden with floor-to-ceiling arched windows. In the center of the room, three long tables with chairs had been arranged, reminding me of a courtroom with spots for a judge, defendant, and prosecutor.

Ceiling fans moved with languid grace, sending a light breeze down to tickle the hairs that had escaped my ponytail.

"Since the situation concerns both the death and accusation of a member of the League, and a mortal being, we are working with the Watch to come to a resolution," Alasdair told me, holding out chairs for Pixie and me before moving to my right, where three chairs were clustered around a small round table.

Adam entered with the other man, and my heart sank when they moved over to the wall opposite Alasdair, taking seats on a long row of chairs.

"Witnesses," I murmured to Pixie when she glared at Adam. "Although I suspect that other man is with the Watch, possibly the person he has to report to in Turkey."

"What's Adam doing there? He's supposed to be on our side," she whispered back. "He's not supposed to be working with the enemy."

"The Watch isn't the enemy, and I'm pretty sure that he's trying to adopt a neutral stance so that his testimony will carry more weight than if he was obviously supporting us."

She gave one of her derisive half snorts, and pulled out her phone to take a picture of Adam. The flash caught his attention, and he looked first startled, then martyred (again) when she continued to glare at him.

Two more people entered, both women, one of whom wore a gauze sundress with bright red poppies, a crown of red-and-blue flowers on her head, and little bells that tinkled when she walked. The woman in front of her wore a dark blue power suit, the kind with big shoulder pads, aggressive-cut lapels on the jacket, and a skirt that ended just above her knees. They both went to the table in the front, and took seats that faced us.

"Officials, no doubt," I whispered to Pixie. "Probably Watch. Here to listen to the evidence."

"Are they both cops?" she asked, lifting her phone and taking a picture of them, too.

The power suit woman, in the middle of conversing with the flower child, paused to shoot Pixie an unfriendly look.

"Your guess is as good as mine," I answered.

The door opened again, and Rennie entered in the company of a man and a woman. The woman was clearly part of the Watch, since she kept a hand on Rennie's arm. The latter stopped before the empty table, turned to face me, and, to my horror, spat.

It missed both Pixie and me, but the Watch lady wasn't any too pleased, and shoved her down into a chair with a warning to not cause any problems.

"Karma Marx?" the power suit woman asked, looking straight at me.

"Yes, that's me," I said, struggling to get to my feet. My ribs, which had been tightly wrapped by a local healer, gave a scream of protest, but I knew from the previous times I'd been called before officials that it was better to stand.

Power Suit nodded, and spent a few seconds considering Pixie, who was taking more pictures of her. "Are you having a documentary film made of your life?"

"No, this is Pixie O'Hara, my ward, placed in my charge by the Home for Innocents," I said, waggling my hand at Pixie, who, with a roll of her eyes, set down her phone.

Power Suit pursed her lips, but said nothing more to us. She turned to the other table. "Renata Taylor?"

"Present," Rennie said, not bothering to stand. "Against my will, I should add. Illegally detained."

"Magistrate Heather will rule on your complaints," Power Suit snapped, before facing Adam. "You are Adam Dirgesinger?"

Adam rose and made a slight bow that was de rigueur in the Otherworld. "I am."

"Very well." She glanced over at Alasdair, who, in anticipation, was standing. "The magistrate extends cordial greetings to Mr. Durrell, who is well-known to us."

Alasdair made a similar bow to Adam's, although not as smooth. "The magistrate is all courtesy, as ever."

The flower child smiled and winked at him.

"We will now hear the complaints lodged against Renata Taylor by the Watch, on behalf of Karma Marx." Power Suit sat down.

"That hippie is the boss?" Pixie asked so softly I almost couldn't hear it.

"I guess so. No more pictures until this is over, please. We don't need to antagonize anyone."

"The charge laid against Ms. Taylor by the Watch is twofold: first, that she murdered her husband, a mortal, by the name of Alan Taylor, and second, that she attempted murder on Ms. Marx. How would you like to answer those charges, Ms. Taylor?" the magistrate named Heather asked. She had a light voice, the kind that reminded me of 1970s folk singers, all breathy and lilting with a slight accent that I had a hard time pinpointing. French? Italian? Maybe Spanish?

"I am innocent of both charges," Rennie said, waving a hand in dismissal. "In fact, I'm the victim here. That woman's boyfriend assaulted me."

"You were trying to smash my head in with a bottle of champagne," I said, too outraged to keep quiet. Adam looked even more martyred, and tried to send me looks that warned me against speaking without being asked, but I'd been summoned to face charges in the past, and I wasn't going to stand around and let myself be railroaded into a third wergeld. "Adam pulled you off me so that you didn't kill me. That's not assault!"

"He hurt me!" she snapped. "He put a Bête Noire on me, and mistreated me to the point where I have bruises. See?" She pulled up the sleeve of a shirt and displayed a faint purple mark on her upper arm.

"Pixie?" I said, holding my right arm up as high as I could, which was about shoulder-level.

"On it," she said, getting up to move to my right side, where she pulled up the hem of my shirt to expose the bandages wrapped around my torso.

"You broke two of my ribs and bruised several more," I told Rennie. "So you can shove—"

"I believe that what Ms. Marx means is that she was injured by direct actions of the defendant," Adam said, taking a step forward, his eyes on Heather, but I could feel him being annoyed at me.

I nodded at Pixie, who dropped my shirt, and with another grimace of pain, I sat down in the chair.

"You are the witness that was noted in the report?" Heather asked without looking at the few sheets of paper that Power Suit slid across the table.

"I am. And I can say that although I regret that my actions may have caused Ms. Taylor discomfort, it took some effort to stop her from continuing the assault she was conducting upon Ms. Marx's person."

"I think I'd better hear this from the start," Heather said, sending another little smile at Alasdair, who waggled his eyebrows in return.

The next hour was spent with the three of us—Rennie, Adam, and me—telling our stories. I hesitated to spill everything concerning the Akashic League, but figured I'd have to tell Alasdair in the end, and since he was in a fairly happy mood what with the light flirtation going on between him and Heather, he might as well hear the whole thing.

It wasn't until I presented Rennie's phone as evidence that her lawyer spoke up. "We would respectfully like to object to the presentation of the phone as evidence. It belongs to Ms. Taylor, who did not give Ms. Marx permission to either confiscate it or peruse the contents."

"Like hell she didn't," I said, a little surprised by the words coming out of my mouth. I put it down to the drugs I'd received eight hours earlier, when we'd rolled into Istanbul and Adam hustled me off to receive medical attention. Maybe I shouldn't have taken half a pill right before the proceedings… "She told me to find the phone, and then gave me permission to watch the videos on it. *Explicit* permission."

"I did not," Rennie lied.

"You very much did so," I countered.

"Magistrate, as you can see, it is Ms. Marx's word against my client's," the lawyer said.

Pixie took a picture of him, then said in a level of voice intended to be overheard, "I'm so posting him on the Reddit Asshat Lawyers subgroup."

"Actually, since Rennie—sorry, Ms. Taylor—died, her property at the time of her death passed to her husband, which makes the phone part of his estate. And since this investigation is regarding his death, it seems reasonable to include its contents as evidence," I said with as much serenity as I could manufacture. The pain meds were starting to kick in, making me relaxed and a bit loopy feeling, but not so much that I couldn't adopt a serious mien.

"She has a point," Heather told the lawyer.

He sputtered out some half-assed objection, but I didn't pay too much attention to it. I was suddenly caught by the way the light streaming in the window was flirting with the side of Adam's face, caressing his cheek, tenderly sweeping along his ear, and throwing itself willy-nilly along the tantalizing curve of his lower lip.

Adam, who had been watching the lawyer, cast a glance my way, did a double take when I sent him a come-hither look, and then closed his eyes for a few seconds, his well-worn martyred expression back in view.

Heather ruled in favor of listening to the phone recordings, and did so. Rennie looked first annoyed, then smug.

"She thinks she's won," I whispered to Pixie.

"She so hasn't."

I nodded, but I wasn't too sure. We had her dead to rights on the assault, but where we were lacking was a reason for her wanting Alan dead, let alone how he'd died. Adam had given him a brief examination noting he'd been stabbed several times.

"Let me see if I have the facts," Heather said after what seemed like an interminable amount of time, but which the clock above Adam said was really seven minutes. "You, Ms. Taylor, deny any knowledge of the reason Ms. Marx said she was sent to find you."

"That's right. I was just taking a trip with my husband."

"While dead," I said. "And your husband had no idea you were there, because you were careful to never let him see you."

Adam shot me a warning look, but I decided it was better not to acknowledge it. I knew the pain meds were lowering some of my inhibitions, but I would be damned if I let anyone railroad me.

"I'm an Alastor," she snapped. "I have a corporeal form."

"Right, but you're still a spirit. And that brings the question of just who raised you." I tapped my lips, a piece of the puzzle that was Rennie sliding into place. I turned to ask Alasdair, "Did you know that Rennie's good friend Lori—the one who sent me on this trip with a tale about Rennie in such a dire situation that I couldn't refuse to help—did you know that Lori has the ability to raise a spirit? She was trained as a necromancer."

"Objection!" Rennie leaped to her feet. "That's not pertinent."

Her lawyer sighed. "Would you please let me handle the objections?"

"You're not doing your job," she said in a near snarl. "It's not your ass that's on the line here."

He was about to protest, but before he could, Heather said, "I would like to know who raised you to be an Alastor rather than, say, a normal spirit. Or even a lich."

Alasdair had been looking at his phone during that exchange, and after it pinged a few times, he looked up and said, "As a matter of fact, Ms. Marx is correct. The individual in question apprenticed as a necromancer, but later gave that up in order to take a managerial position."

"Booyah! The defense rests its case." Pixie jumped to her feet again before slamming her hand on the table, then quickly sitting down.

"Actually, we're not the defense, not for this case, and we aren't done," I told her.

"Oh." She rose and lifted her chin. "The not-defense does not rest it's not-case. Thank you."

Heather looked amused. Power Suit came perilously close to rolling her eyes.

Things got a little out of hand at that point, but in the end, Heather passed down the order for the Watch to retain custody of Rennie on grounds of assault, with a pending investigation into the death of Alan.

Rennie's counterclaims against Adam and me were dismissed.

"This is bullshit!" Rennie screamed as she was more or less hauled out of the room, her face red with anger. "It was self-defense! She's sleeping with that man, and they're working together to blame me for everything."

"I have never had sex with him," I said, getting to my feet and nodding toward Adam. "Not that I don't want to, but we haven't."

"Karma, I don't think anyone wants to hear about our private situation—" Adam started to say.

I pointed at Rennie as she was being marched out of the room. "She clearly does. And I'm not going to have your good name besmirched. You're too good a cop to suffer that."

Heather and Power Suit decamped from the front table, making way for Alasdair, who stood at it now, watching us with a sort of long-suffering patience that I expected came from heading up such a big chunk of the League.

"I think I'll forgo having you repeat your statement regarding your experience with Ms. Taylor," he said when Rennie was at last removed, and Heather—with one final flutter of her eyelashes at Alasdair—left with Power Suit.

Only Adam, Pixie, and I were left in the room with Alasdair, the other Watch member having walked out with the others.

"Good, because the pain medicine I took earlier is making me feel like I'm made of flan," I told him.

"Mmm. Flan," Pixie murmured.

"I do love a good flan," Alasdair told her. "I had a delicious bacon flan Cubano last year. It was so good, I ate four servings. Was sick as a dog the next day, but it was worth it."

"Bacon flan? What is this strangeness?" Pixie asked, taking from me my pen and the piece of paper upon which I was doodling. "What sort of bacon? Is it in the flan, or in the caramel sauce?"

Adam leaned forward in his chair and put his head in his hands.

"Candied bacon in the caramel, of course," Alasdair said.

"Of course," Pixie agreed, nodding, and scribbling notes to herself.

"Can we get back to me? Not that I would turn down bacon anything, because at this point, I'm ravenous, but I'm also getting very sleepy."

"Ah. Yes. Just so." He cocked an eyebrow at me. "We have to deal with the violation of your prohibition against the use of exterminations. I'd like to hear in your words what happened."

I told him exactly what transpired, from Olga and Teodor's warning to the point where I'd stopped Hervé from stabbing Pixie.

"I've read the statement you both made to Mr. Dirgesinger regarding the incident with the violent spirit," Alasdair said, his expression no longer friendly and sunny. "Is there anything either of you would like to add?"

"Karma saved my life," Pixie said, crossing all four of her arms. "It was him or me, and she chose me. I'm sixteen. Draw your own conclusion."

"Pixie!" I still had enough wits to send her a warning look. "You don't need to be so antagonistic."

"He wants to throw you into that Akasha place. If you go there, then I'll have to get another foster family, and I'm just not up to that. Do you hear?" She slapped her hands on the table and leaned forward to pin Alasdair back with a long look. "I am not up to it!"

"Oh, goddess—I'm sorry about—"

"No need for apology," he interrupted, getting to his feet. I was a bit floored when he smiled, and added, "I am obligated to refer the matter back to your direct superior and will inform him that our investigation has shown no cause for punitive action. That, coupled with the fact you saved the life of an innocent child, should clear your name of all wrongdoing."

"Woot!" Pixie cheered, doing a few fist pumps.

"Thank you," I said, carefully getting to my feet, grateful for Adam when he moved over with a hand on the uninjured side of my back. "I very much appreciate your support. I was worried that the League would find me unsuitable to continue to foster Pixie."

"I can't speak for the Home," he said, "but if I were in charge of this young lady, I couldn't think of anyone else who was so perfectly poised to teach her the ways of being a TAE."

"We won! We won!" Pixie waited until Alasdair, with a nod to Adam, left us alone in the magnificent room. She did a little spin. "Even if your boss tries to do a number on you, I bet Mr. Head Honcho will tell him a thing or two. Now we can go see Bakirposa Kost."

"The what?" Adam asked, gently guiding me when I weaved a few steps.

"It's a wooden manor house that looks like something straight out of a horror movie. Pixie read about it online and has been dying to see it. I told her we could go on our tourist time here."

"It's even creepier than your house," Pixie said, pulling up a picture on her phone to show Adam.

"Thanks," he said in a tone of voice that made me giggle. "Do you want to go sleep off your pain pills?"

"No, I did enough of that earlier. I'm hungry. Can we go to a café or something?"

We could, and we did. A half hour later we claimed a table on the sidewalk of Istiklal Caddesi, a well-known pedestrian zone in Istanbul filled with restaurants, shops, and even an old school. Buskers dotted street corners playing a variety of music, and the smell wafting out of several of the restaurants had us all salivating.

"I'm so going to make pastries when we get home," Pixie said, licking honey off her fingers from a treat she'd bought at a vendor. "Baklava is definitely on my to-do list."

"It's my Watch boss wanting to talk to me about your complaint against the necromancer Lori. Be back in a couple. Order for me," Adam said when his phone went off, and moved over to a quieter section of the street.

"Tell him I hope that Lori gets some sort of punishment for her role in Alan's death," I called after him. He raised a hand to let me know he heard me.

"Why would I want to be you?" Pixie asked a minute later, startling me as I was reading the menu posted on the café wall.

"What?"

"That Alasdair dude. He said the League would want me to stay with you to learn to be an exterminator."

"Ah. That." I sat back, enjoying the heat coming off the pavement, as well as the sights and sounds of the tourists and inhabitants who strolled up and down the street. Languages varying from Turkish to Arabic, English, and even some Italian drifted around us. "That's most likely because they realize that you are special."

"Of course I am." She waggled both hands, her glamour keeping her extra arms hidden.

"Beyond that. You can see spirits. Not everyone can, you know, and the fact that you can means that you may well have abilities that align with being a TAE."

She frowned. "What if I don't want to kill ghosts?"

"I don't kill them, as you very well know, and if you don't want to learn the art of extermination, then you don't have to. You could become a chef."

"And be at the beck and call of entitled people? No thank you." She pushed her phone an inch. "I'll think about it, but I'm not promising anything."

"You have plenty of time to make the decision of what you want to do with your life," I told her, feeling like a cat that had found a pool of sunshine.

"You didn't," she pointed out.

"No, but I'm special."

"You can say that again."

The man's voice that spoke came from my left, causing me to skew around in my chair, which in turn made my ribs protest.

"Ow!" I squawked, flinching at the stab of pain, then opening my eyes when I saw who'd spoken. "Um. Hello."

"Hello," Alan Taylor said, glancing from me to Pixie. "I see you haven't been banished."

"No. Not that your wife didn't do everything she could to see that happen."

He made a face. "Ex-wife. Well, deceased wife. Deceased former wife."

"What are you doing here?" I asked. "I assume someone raised you?"

"Summoned, yes. The local fellow with your Akashic League arranged for it. Turns out the Watch asked him to help since they wanted to have a chat about what happened with Rennie, and as I was agreeable, here I am." He looked around the street. "Seems pleasant enough being dead. At least this way I don't have to worry about Rennie doing something to harm others. She was quite mad, you know. I thought it was all over when she died in the car accident that was supposed to kill me but ended up destroying her. Then she returned, and she and her friend continued their plans to get me out of the picture so they could take over my business."

"She died in an accident?" I asked. "You didn't … er …"

"Kill her?" He looked offended, and rightly so, given that my verbal filter appeared to be completely missing. "Of course not! She was off her rocker, but I would never have resorted to violence."

"I heard a recording … oh. You said she had tried something, but that it failed. She had tried to do you in before?"

"A few times," he said with a shrug. "I was in the process of divorcing her when she pulled the last stunt. The one that got her killed instead of me."

"If she and Lori were in it together … then they sent me after you … why?" I asked, rubbing my head.

Alan shrugged again, and stepped aside when a bright red trolley trundled its way past. "From what I'd guess, she was going to use you as a scapegoat, someone to foist the blame onto for my death once she finally managed that. Which she did by drugging me, then stabbing me eight times."

"Deus!" Pixie said.

I knew just how she felt.

Alan looked around again, his angry expression easing. "She got me in the end, but now that I see how nice the afterlife is, I don't really mind. All I ever really wanted to do was travel, and now I can do so. The Summoner who raised me said I can go anywhere so long as I have sufficient rest to interact with the mortal world."

"Congratulations. Er … I hate to seem all Agatha Christie wrapping up at the end of a book, but can you tell me why you were so angry with me? I wasn't trying to harm you."

"No, but you were clearly in Rennie's sights, and she'd somehow fooled you. I kept telling you to leave her alone, but you wouldn't listen." His voice was filled with both irritation and annoyance. "Anyone who knew her would realize that sooner or later she'd turn on you, but you just wouldn't listen, would you?"

Pixie started to bristle on my behalf, but I simply smiled and said, "I believed what Rennie told me. At first, that is."

"And that's where you went wrong," he said, biting off each word before taking a deep breath. "Well, I'm off to see the city. Think I might go into incorporeal form and take a plane to Athens next. Always did want to make a tour of the Mediterranean."

He strolled across the street, pausing to look at a shop.

"Since we're doing Agatha Christie Wrap-Up Time, how did you know that it was Rennie and not Alan who attacked you?" Pixie asked.

"Hmm?" I gave myself a mental shake, not wanting to doze off in public. "Oh, she told me Alan knew I stole the phone. That was simply not true."

"OK, but *how* did you know that?" she asked.

"Because I'd searched the bag that Rennie claimed the phone was in. By that point, I realized something was up because nowhere in any of the bags in Alan's compartment was there women's clothing. Or cosmetics, or even common toiletries. It was all Alan's stuff. No one else mentioned Rennie, and she hardly ever appeared in the lounge car. All of which meant she was making very specific appearances, and the only spirit who could do that and who could pass for the living was an Alastor. Oh, look, it's Donna and her sisters."

"And Olga and Teodor," Pixie said, quickly getting to her feet. "I'm going to go get pictures of them before they fade away. Don't eat my food!"

I sat in silence for a minute, watching idly as Pixie took several pictures against a scenic building, Olga and Teodor happily posing for her. Just as I was about to drift off, a shadow fell over me, causing me to jerk up in my seat.

Pain lacing my side woke me up fast enough. "If it isn't my fair fellow traveler," Rev said, beaming as he paused next to me, his arms laden with bags. "Enjoying Istanbul?"

"Very much so," I told him, then politely gestured to a chair. "Would you like to join us for lunch?"

"No, no, I'm meeting a fellow clergyman in half an hour, but if you wouldn't mind, I would relish the opportunity to sit for a few minutes. All this walking, you know …"

"I completely understand. It's a gorgeous city, but a bit hard on the feet," I agreed.

We chatted for a few minutes about the city, but the whole time, I had a feeling he was watching me closely. More closely than was strictly warranted.

Olga and Teodor drifted past, the former blowing me a kiss while the latter waved.

Rev turned to look when I gave them a smile and little nod.

"Tell me," I said, pouring a glass of sparkling water and pushing it toward him. "How long have you been able to see ghosts?"

He hesitated as he reached for the glass, his eyes considering me with an unusually grave mien. "Since I was a lad."

"So you saw Rennie?"

"Rennie?"

"Alan Taylor's wife."

"Ah. The brown woman." He gave a little waggle of his eyebrows as he sipped his water. "I didn't actually see her, not as I suspect you did. To me, spirits appear as patches of glimmering light. Sometimes that light forms into a human shape; other times it's just a faint sparkle in the air. Just now, for instance, I saw a blue sparkle next to you, and I couldn't help but wonder why that was."

"Mr. Taylor stopped by to tell me his plans."

"Poor man," he said, his face solemn. Adam had told me that the Watch—in the guise of local police— had informed the train officials that Alan had died in his sleep. "I take it he's found peace?"

"I think so," I said, watching as Alan tried on a hat from a rack of clothing outside a boutique. "He said he was looking forward to traveling."

Rev's eyebrows rose. "Ghosts can ... er ..."

"Some can, yes."

"And you? You're one of the special ones, too?" he asked in a polite but fairly pointed manner.

"You could say that. Like you, I've seen ghosts since I was a child. Only I see them as more than just sparkles."

"You are truly blessed," he said, nodding.

Adam crossed the street to join Pixie, who was poring over a tray of jewelry sold by a secondhand shop. He pulled out his wallet and passed a few bills over to the vendor, earning him a quick hug from Pixie before she draped herself with several strands of Victorian black beads.

"Yes," I said, smiling, feeling for the first time in many days like life was filled with infinite possibilities. "I really am."

EPILOGUE

Deus! Will you stop worrying? I'm fine! Nothing happened. Well, stuff happened, but Karma was there, and she went all badass on the guy who tried to stab me in the throat, so there's no need to make me talk out the trauma.

Also, Karma said you can't put me with any other foster people, because I can see spirits, and she's the only one around who can teach me how to do what she does, which is kind of cool, because I would have totally banished that asshat if I could have. Besides, Karma didn't do anything wrong, so you can't say that she's not a good influence. I mean, she's not all that, but she is OK enough, and lets me cook, and says she'll pay for a culinary course at the local college if that's what I want to do. And she needs me. She has all those imps, and people are always taking advantage of her, so she needs me to keep an eye on things.

Yes, her boyfriend is here, but you got the wrong idea about what I said. It's not like they're doing anything in front of me other than kissing every now and again, and even then, it's not, like, with tongues or anything. They like each other, and it's not fair for you to say that they are behaving inappropriately in front of me. You're not here, so you don't know! The crazy ghost—the second one, not the one who tried to kill me—almost beat in her head, and ended up breaking her ribs, so she (Karma) can't even get it on with Adam right now. Yeah, they sleep in the same bed, but Adam told Karma they weren't going to do anything until she got a note from her doctor saying she could, at which point she yelled at him that she was the one who got to say when she could do sexy times, not a doctor, and then Adam told her that he was only thinking of her, and then they didn't talk to each other for a couple of hours until I pointed out to them they were being idiots.

Then Karma laughed, and Adam said he wasn't trying to take autonomy away from her, but that he was concerned, and then they did kiss—but not with tongues—and we all went out to see the best haunted house ever, except Karma wouldn't let me go in because she said it looks condemned. Adam and I went around the back and snuck into the kitchen, but he wouldn't let me go farther because the floor was rotted.

Karma needs me. Adam kind of needs me, mostly to help him with Karma. So everything is fine, and I don't want to leave, and I'm going to make bacon flan Cubano when I get home.

I have to go. There's a doll shop near our hotel, and I saw a bunch of outfits that would fit Karma's imps, and I'm going to get some for her for a late birthday present.

I'm fine, OK? Deus! Just stop worrying! I've got Karma and Adam, and nothing is going to happen with them around.

To: Pixie O'Hara

Famous last words, my dear. I'll see you on the seventh at your regular time. Please bring recipe for bacon flan Cubano.

Dr. Felicity Wellbottom

NOTE TO READERS

My lovely one! I hope you enjoyed reading this book, which I handcrafted from the finest artisanal words just for you. If you are one of the folks who likes to review books, I'd love it if you posted a review for it on your favorite book spot (be sure to tell me if you do, so that I can lavish praise all over you).

If you're looking for some fun behind-the-scenes tidbits and exclusive material available free just for you via Bookfunnel, hie thee over to my website at katiemacalister.com and sign up for the newsletter.

Did you enjoy the tale of Karma, Pixie, and Adam? Want more? Luckily, the first book in the series, *Ghost of a Chance*, is available. You can dip into the first chapter by popping over to my website (URL above).

ABOUT THE AUTHOR

For as long as she can remember, Katie MacAlister has loved reading. Growing up in a family where a weekly visit to the library was a given, Katie spent much of her time with her nose buried in a book.

Two years after she started writing novels, Katie sold her first romance, *Noble Intentions*. More than seventy books later, her novels have been translated into numerous languages, been recorded as audiobooks, received several awards, and have been regulars on the *New York Times, USA Today, Publishers Weekly*, and *Wall Street Journal* bestseller lists. Katie lives in the Pacific Northwest with two dogs, and can often be found lurking around online.

You are welcome to join Katie's official discussion group on Facebook, as well as connect with her via TikTok and Instagram. For more information, visit her website at www.katiemacalister.com